Phoenix, Upside Down

by
ELIZABETH SCARBORO

VIKING

J/Scarboro

I would like to thank my close friends and family members for giving me honest critiques, interesting perspectives, and the support that kept me going. I also owe deep thanks to two teachers: Betsy Hearne, who was the godmother of my first book; and Anne Dyson, who showed me what it means to consider a child's point of view.

Finally, I would like to thank Elizabeth Law, my editor at Viking, who has given me encouragement and insight throughout. —E.S.

VIKING
Published by the Penguin Group
Penguin Books USA Inc., 375 Hudson Street, New York, New York 10014, U.S.A.
Penguin Books Ltd, 27 Wrights Lane, London W8 5TZ, England
Penguin Books Australia Ltd, Ringwood, Victoria, Australia
Penguin Books Canada Ltd, 10 Alcorn Avenue, Toronto, Ontario, Canada M4V 3B2
Penguin Books (N.Z.) Ltd, 182–190 Wairau Road, Auckland 10, New Zealand

Penguin Books Ltd, Registered Offices: Harmondsworth, Middlesex, England

First published in 1996 by Viking, a division of Penguin Books USA Inc.

1   3   5   7   9   10   8   6   4   2

LIBRARY OF CONGRESS CATALOGING-IN-PUBLICATION DATA
Scarboro, Elizabeth.
Phoenix, upside down / by Elizabeth Scarboro.   p.   cm.
Summary : Jamie moves with her family to Phoenix where she and her sister are the "new kids" at school and where they befriend an older woman who helps Jamie adjust
ISBN 0-670-86335-1
[1. Moving, Household—Fiction.   2. Sisters—Fiction.   3. Schools—Fiction.]   I. Title.
PZ7.S3237Ph   1996   [Fic]—dc20   95-47236   CIP   AC

Manufactured in U.S.A.
Set in Garamond

For Mom, Dad, Catherine, John, and Jean:
from the Blue River to Wolverine Lake
And for Stephen:
from Kirby Coves to Orlando's Bench

Chapter One

Jamie felt the heat rush into the car. She sat up in the backseat and looked out the window, expecting to see a fire, but there were no flames. The empty road stretched out straight in front of them, and the only thing rising up from its sides was dust.

Jamie leaned close to the front seat.

"Maybe we should roll up the windows," she said, "and try to keep the heat out."

"Jamie! Glad to hear you've gotten your voice back," her dad said, catching her eye in the rearview mirror.

"The air will only get hotter if we don't let it circulate," her mom answered.

Jamie sat back in her seat. She'd vowed not to talk to her parents for the whole ride to Phoenix, since they were making her go. She'd been quiet the entire first day, but now that they were getting closer there were a few things she needed to know.

"Is it going to be this hot in Phoenix?" she asked.

"It's hotter than this down there," her mom said. "But the houses are all air-conditioned."

Jamie had never wanted air-conditioning before. In Colorado, if she got too hot, all she had to do was open the window. But that was Colorado. And now she just had one more thing to make her hate leaving it behind.

Jamie looked over at her sister Rachel, who was lying next to her, curled up against the door. She was sound asleep, ignoring the heat. Even though Rachel was two years younger, she had figured out how to sleep through the worst parts of car rides.

Jamie glanced down at the seat on her other side, and peered into her pet rat Spotsey's cage. She watched Spotsey dig himself deeper into his cedar chips as he slept. He reminded Jamie of a soccer ball curled up like that, with his black spots spreading out through his white fur.

Spotsey lifted his head to yawn and stretched out his front paws. Soon he'd feel the heat, Jamie was sure. The glass walls of his cage were already warm. Quietly, Jamie lifted the cage's wire lid off .

"Come here, Spots," she leaned down to tell him. He

climbed on top of her hand and she lifted him onto her lap.

On the car seat, Spotsey looked around slowly, still half-asleep. He reminded Jamie of the way he had looked when he'd been a tiny baby. He'd stare up from his food bowl the way he stared now, like he'd been brought to a foreign planet.

Spotsey was bigger now, but he was still pretty cute. Jamie's best friend Sheila would come over just to visit him. She and Jamie spent whole afternoons building mazes and towers out of wooden blocks for Spotsey. Jamie wondered if Spotsey would miss Sheila, now that he'd be spending a year in Arizona.

"Jamie," her mom said, "Did you take Spotsey out?"

"Yeah, but he's only sitting in my lap. He won't go anywhere."

Her mom turned around and glanced from Spotsey to Jamie. She raised one eyebrow. Jamie held Spotsey closer.

"The last thing we need is an escaped rat," she said.

"He listens to me," Jamie said. "Besides, he's tired."

She leaned back against the seat and stared out the window. Dust and more dust.

The car slowed down. Jamie saw the top of a McDonald's *M,* followed by a gas station, then a stoplight.

"Where are we?" Rachel asked, her eyes still closed.

"Flagstaff," their dad said.

Jamie sat up. There were actually some mountains behind the town, and they looked a little bit like the mountains at home, except they were much smaller.

"It's a little cooler up here," her mom said. "Maybe this is a good place to stop and stretch."

"It would be nice to get to Phoenix before dark," her dad said.

"We can still make it," her mom answered. "We'll just stop for fifteen minutes or so."

"Fifteen minutes means half an hour," her dad sighed. But they stopped at the edge of a large park that had a few picnic tables and a grassy field lined with trees.

"Come on," Rachel said.

"Just a sec," Jamie said. "I've got to get Spotsey ready."

She scooted out after Rachel, holding Spotsey close to her stomach.

"Spotsey can stay right here," her mom said.

"Can't I take him to the park?" Jamie asked. "I always take him outside at home."

"Jamie," her mom said.

"Come on Mom, how would you like to be in a cage for two days in a row?"

"Jamie?" Her mom sounded like she might decide to leave Jamie in the car along with Spotsey.

"Please, Mom? It's only for a minute, then I'll put him back."

Her mom sighed.

"Don't let go of him. We're not going to spend the afternoon chasing that rat through Flagstaff."

Jamie glanced down at Spotsey. She couldn't argue with that. Her mom had already helped her search for Spotsey once this week, in Jamie's room. When her mom had opened Jamie's dresser drawer, Spotsey had stuck his head out from behind her socks, making her mom jump halfway to the ceiling.

Jamie put Spotsey down near the bottom of a huge tree. He dug at the grass, stretching his back.

"He looks better outside," Rachel said.

"I know," Jamie said. "He looks so sick when we're driving."

"I know how he feels," Rachel said. "I keep thinking I'm going to throw up. I even feel sick in my dreams."

"I told you moving to Arizona was going to be terrible," Jamie said.

"This isn't moving," Rachel said. "This is just the car ride."

Jamie glared at Rachel. Hadn't she noticed that they were already in Arizona, and that it was too hot to stand?

"Once we get to our new house it'll be fun." Rachel smirked. "We might never even want to go back."

Jamie groaned. Rachel had to miss Colorado, after two days of being gone. Jamie counted on that. She knew they were moving so her dad could try out a new job for a year. Her parents hadn't decided whether they wanted to stay for just this year, or move for good. Jamie needed Rachel's help to convince them that a year was all they needed away from their real home.

"You'll want to go back," Jamie said. "It's even hotter than this in Phoenix."

"We can go swimming," Rachel said.

"Girls," their dad called to them, "if you want to run around before we start again, now's the time to do it."

Rachel started running.

"It's a race!" she said.

"No fair starting before you call the race," Jamie yelled. She scooped up Spotsey and ran after her sister.

Back in the car, Jamie wiped the sweat off her forehead. She glanced down at Spotsey. He was lying in her lap, his eyes closed.

"I think Spotsey's too hot," Jamie said.

"Poor guy," her dad said. "He's had to adjust to a big change in temperature."

"I'm hot, too," Rachel said.

"We're almost at the Harrisons'," her dad said.

Jamie closed her eyes. She could hear her parents talking quietly in the front seat. They talked quietly a lot lately, and she knew they were talking about moving. The first few times, she'd tried to listen, but now she was sick of picturing her new house and wondering how long they'd live there. She and Rachel had only brought a few toys and books, and Jamie was sure they'd be bored before the first week was over.

The car slowed to a stop.

"I can't believe it," Rachel said. "It seemed like we were never going to get there."

Their mom turned around.

"Jamie, why don't we take Spotsey inside with us and let him cool off," she said.

"Okay," Jamie said. She was glad her mom had remembered to think about Spotsey. She helped her mom carry Spotsey's cage through the Harrisons' door. They set it down on a table in the front hallway and followed the Harrisons into the kitchen.

"Jamie," Mr. Harrison said, "you brought Spotsey all this way?"

"Are you kidding?" Mrs. Harrison said. "He's a member of the family by now. If he'd stayed in Boulder, Jamie probably would have stayed with him."

Jamie smiled. She had threatened her parents with that just a few days ago, when they'd wanted her to give him away. The only person she'd consider giving him to would be Sheila, and Sheila's mom had said no before Sheila finished asking.

"So how was the trip?" Mrs. Harrison asked.

"It was good," Jamie's mom said, "except for a few small things."

Jamie knew she was one of those small things, after not talking for a day. That morning, when she sat silently after Rachel asked her a question, she caught the look on her mom's face in the rearview mirror. For a second she felt bad, but then she changed her mind. Her silence was nothing compared to moving someone away from her home.

"You must be hungry," Mr. Harrison said. "We have lasagna waiting for you."

Jamie hadn't realized she was hungry until she sat down at the kitchen table and saw her plate of lasagna. She and Rachel began eating while her parents sat on the couch.

"Do you have chocolate ice cream?" Rachel asked, beating Jamie to the question.

"Rachel!" their dad hissed.

Mrs. Harrison laughed.

"She remembers!" she said. "The month I lived at your

house, when Roger was out here, I never went a night without chocolate ice cream."

Jamie had liked having Mrs. Harrison around. She was more of an older sister than a grown-up, and she even held Spotsey sometimes.

Jamie looked up from her lasagna.

"I'll be right back," she said. "I have to check Spotsey's water."

She walked into the hallway and glanced at Spotsey's water bottle. It was still half full.

"You probably hate warm water, don't you," she said.

Then she looked closer. Spotsey was standing very still, halfway in and halfway out of the empty peanut-butter jar he slept in. Something about the way he stood made Jamie scared to pet him. She put her hand down in his cage.

"Come here, Spots," she said.

But he couldn't hear her.

Jamie leaned down close to him and petted his back. It was stiff under her fingers. She lifted him up out of the cage and held him close to her. His eyes stared back at her, unchanging, as quiet as the rest of him.

"What happened?" Jamie whispered to him, putting him close to her face, trying to wake him up with her breathing.

She could feel the tears building up behind her eyes. She

didn't want to go back into the kitchen. She only wanted to talk to Spotsey, and that was the one thing she couldn't do.

"Jamie?" her dad came into the hallway.

"Dad, look," she said. "He's dead."

"Oh, Jamie," he said, putting his arm around her, "I'm sorry."

"What happened?" Jamie asked into his shirt.

"I don't know," her dad said. "Maybe he just couldn't take the change in temperature."

Jamie imagined Spotsey sweating in the car, then shivering when they brought him inside. If they were at home, Spotsey would never have felt the heat, or the air-conditioning. He'd be running around her room right now, messing with her socks. But they were here, and he was gone, leaving her to live in the same heat that had taken him far away.

"I'm sorry, Spotsey," Jamie said. She wanted to tell him more, but everything sounded strange and her throat was beginning to ache. As she lifted him back into his cage the ache spread all the way through her. Her dad hugged her with both arms now, and she let herself be buried inside his soft, white T-shirt.

Chapter Two

Jamie woke to a shaking thud. She wondered if Rachel would ever get tired of falling out of the top bunk in their new room. It couldn't be that much fun, especially in the morning, but Rachel insisted it was even better than jumping.

Jamie lay turned to the wall, listening to Rachel open her dresser drawer.

"It's the first day of school today," Rachel hummed to herself. "I get to wear my sandals."

Rachel had already unpacked her boxes and folded her clothes in piles. Jamie made fun of her, but this morning it might have been nice to have clothes waiting in piles. She had things to think about, and she didn't feel like digging through her big box until she found something to wear.

"We're going to school today," Rachel said, in the voice their parents used to make them hurry.

"I know," Jamie said to her pillow. "I just want to sleep a little more."

"I can't hear you," Rachel hummed, sorting through her piles.

Jamie tried to crawl back inside her dream. A woman wearing a large brown hat was fishing, casting her line into a rushing river. Jamie was about to see her face when she was interrupted by a rustling sound. Rachel was getting dressed.

"Okay, okay," Jamie said. She sat up on her bed, staying huddled over so she wouldn't hit her head on the bunk above her. She watched Rachel leave the room heading toward the kitchen, still humming her made-up song.

Jamie got up and looked into her box. She wormed her hand down through her clothes until she felt her T-shirt with faded purple flowers.

Jamie wandered into the kitchen.

Rachel looked up from her cereal.

"Aren't you going to wear a dress?"

Jamie made her own bowl of cereal.

"I like this shirt," she said. "It's better than any dress."

"But it's the first day of school," Rachel said. She stared at their parents, who were sitting on the bench across from her at the table.

"Slide over," Jamie said, glaring at Rachel as she put her

cereal down on the table. What if kids *did* dress up in Phoenix for the first day of school? But usually only the younger kids dressed up, because their parents made them. By the time kids got to fourth grade it was a different story.

"It's different for you," Jamie told Rachel. "Besides, you'd wear a dress no matter what day it was."

"Girls," their mom interrupted slowly, as she lifted her coffee cup.

Jamie kicked Rachel lightly under the table as she ate her cereal.

"We need to leave in a few minutes," her dad reminded them.

Rachel smirked at Jamie behind her dad's back and then squirmed past her, leaving the bench to get her backpack. Before Jamie had rinsed her bowl, Rachel was already by the front door, skipping back and forth while she waited for Jamie and her dad.

Jamie picked up her backpack. She was glad her dad had offered to walk them to the bus stop today. When Jamie was really little, her dad used to walk with her to school the whole way. She wondered if going to school on the bus would start to seem shorter after a while. For now it was all she could do not to hold her dad's hand as the three of them left the house.

———

Jamie stood outside Room 408. She had been searching for her room since she'd found Rachel's, telling herself she wouldn't be late. She'd counted on slipping in quietly and raising her hand quickly when the teacher called her name. But now the bell had rung. She would have to walk over to the teacher in front of the whole class and explain that she was new. Last year, Rebecca Small had barely stepped into the classroom before she'd had to tell the class about moving to Colorado from Kansas. She'd stood up alone in front of all of them, looking like she belonged somewhere else.

Jamie's stomach jumped. She felt like she was on the high dive looking down, staring into the water. She caught her breath and wiped the sweat off her forehead. With one quick jerk, she opened the door.

"Ah ha!" Jamie's teacher whirled around to face her, smiling like she'd just uncovered a mysterious clue.

"Let me guess . . . Jamie?"

Jamie nodded. Mrs. Hazelett looked like a Mrs. Hazelett. She had dark eyes, and lipstick that didn't stay in the lines. Her teeth jumped out from behind her maroon lips.

"I was beginning to wonder if you were going to be in my class after all," she told Jamie.

"I didn't know where the room was," Jamie mumbled.

"It's confusing," Mrs. Hazelett said. She turned to the rest of the class. "I'm sure all of you had the same problem when you first came here."

Jamie didn't bother to see if the kids were nodding. She was going to have plenty of time to look at them soon enough.

"Jamie came here all the way from Colorado," Mrs. Hazelett said. "I'm sure you'll all help her get to know her way around here at Lookout Elementary."

Jamie glanced past Mrs. Hazelett's head out the window. The playground was empty, and the tetherballs looked lonely, hanging still against their poles.

"Jamie," Mrs. Hazelett was saying, "you can sit next to Elise."

She pointed to the only empty desk, one of a pair on the left side of the room. Jamie walked over toward it and slid in. The backs of her neck and ears felt hot. They were probably turning red. For the first time since she'd moved, she was glad to have long hair.

Mrs. Hazelett started to speak again. Jamie slumped in her chair. It was over. Mrs. Hazelett hadn't been too bad, though her teeth were definitely too white next to her lipstick. They reminded Jamie of wolves' teeth in cartoons, shining as they chomped their food.

The two girls at the pair of desks in front of Jamie turned around, mouthing silent "hi"s. Jamie mouthed "hi" back. She was relieved to see they were wearing normal clothes like she was. They both had their hair combed neatly into short ponytails. Jamie's mother had tried to braid hers, but she'd squirmed until her mother settled for pulling a little bit into a barrette at the top of her head. That made Jamie feel naked enough. Looking at herself in the mirror, she'd caught a glimpse of her bald grandpa.

Jamie tried to forget about the kids long enough to listen to Mrs. Hazelett.

"It's the first day," she was saying, "so we won't rush into anything. I think we'll start with a story."

Jamie pushed her chair in and got ready to stand in the lunch line. She heard her name, underneath the shuffling of the class. She looked up. Mrs. Hazelett was walking toward her.

"Jamie," she said. "Meet Tanya and Stephanie."

Jamie turned to face the two girls who had been sitting in front of her.

"They're going to show you around and help you get the hang of things today."

"Okay." Jamie nodded.

"Come on." Stephanie smiled. "Let's go get in the lunch line."

Jamie stood between them. As she looked at them closely, she realized that their T-shirts had been ironed and were neatly tucked in. Jamie smoothed the sides of her shorts.

"The cafeteria's really noisy," Tanya said. "We eat at the same time as the kindergartners. Can you believe it?"

"At least we don't have to share tables with them," Stephanie said. "They're so messy."

Jamie wondered what Stephanie would think of her clothes box.

"Yeah," said Tanya. "We weren't like that in kindergarten."

"Have you been here since kindergarten?" Jamie asked her.

"Yeah," they said together.

"We even had the same kindergarten teacher," Tanya said.

"Mr. Shoelace!"

They both burst out laughing.

The line slowed down. Jamie could see the kids ahead of her sticking their hands above a metal bin as they walked.

"What's going on?" Jamie asked Stephanie.

"Some people take forever to wash their hands," she said.

"Hmmm," Jamie said.

Stephanie looked over her shoulder.

"Didn't you have a water line at your school?" she asked.

"No." Jamie watched Stephanie's mouth turn into a straight line.

"I guess it was too cold to have water outside like this," Jamie added. "Our hands would've frozen."

"But you washed your hands, didn't you?" Stephanie stopped to face her.

Jamie tried not to smile. Stephanie would have been horrified to know that the kids at her old school didn't think about washing their hands before lunch.

"Of course," Jamie said. "We just went into the bathroom to do it."

"Oh, I get it," Stephanie said. "Wow, it was that cold, huh?"

"I've been to a place like that," Tanya said from behind. "I went skiing and it was so cold I couldn't take my hands out of my gloves."

"Really?" Stephanie asked.

And they were off talking again, giving Jamie the chance to figure out the water line before she got to the front. It looked easy, but she couldn't help feeling like everyone was watching her to see if she knew what to do. Hopefully, Tanya and Stephanie would just keep talking, and she would glide right through.

Jamie stood in the bus parking lot. It seemed like days had gone by since she'd stood there that morning, helping Rachel figure out how to get to her class. She waited at the edge of the lot, watching kids gather into four different bus lines. They were supposed to stand single file, but everyone stood in twos and threes, talking with their friends. Finally, Jamie went to stand in her line. She watched a group of boys talk in front of her, hoping that the bus would come soon. At her old school, she never cared if people saw her standing alone. Then again, she wasn't alone that often.

She wondered if Rachel had found their bus line yet. She looked up and down the line for another person standing alone, but she didn't see anyone. Then she heard someone calling Rachel's name. She squinted at the girl, who was standing with a big group of girls who were younger than Jamie. Jamie looked at them closely, and soon she saw Rachel, standing in the middle of the group.

Jamie felt the line move forward. As she walked toward the bus, she saw the second-grade girls peeling away from Rachel, heading toward their own bus lines. She couldn't believe it—they'd all been waiting in the wrong line just to keep Rachel company.

Jamie stepped up onto the bus. She heard someone call her name. She didn't need to look up—she'd know Rachel's voice anywhere.

"Over here," Rachel was saying. "I saved you a seat."

Jamie slid in next to her and watched the parking lot begin to roll by. Soon she and Rachel would be walking back to their new house. For once, she looked forward to being there. Compared to Colorado it still seemed too new, but compared to Lookout Elementary, it almost felt like home.

Chapter Three

Jamie sat on her bunk, looking through the pictures she'd taken her last week in Colorado. Most of them had turned out different from the way she'd thought they would. It was only the second time she'd used a camera, and she'd had trouble holding it still.

Sheila had brought the camera when she came over to Jamie's on the weekend before the last day of school. Now Jamie sifted through that day. She stared at Sheila, smiling upside down as she hung from the jungle gym, her stringy brown hair hanging beneath her. Next Sheila was standing on top of the jungle gym, pretending she was about to fall off. Then they were both inside, sitting on Jamie's bed, laughing. Jamie remembered tickling Sheila's side as her mom clicked the camera.

Jamie came to the pictures of the last tower they'd built.

She remembered sorting through the wooden blocks with Sheila, figuring out exactly how they were going to build it. They'd decided to make it two stories high, with a ramp so Spotsey could get from one floor to the other. Sheila had sprinkled Spotsey's food on the roof so that he'd climb all the way to the top.

First there was a picture of just the tower itself. Then Sheila putting Spotsey down next to it. And finally Spotsey sitting by himself, nibbling the food on the roof. Jamie had forgotten how cute he was. The picture made him seem like he was alive somewhere right now, the way Sheila was, and she only had to wait a while before she could see him again.

Jamie ran her fingers over the pictures. She put them down on her bed and hugged her knees, resting her head on her kneecaps. With her eyes closed, she could see Sheila sitting on the white carpet in her old room.

Jamie heard the door creak.

"Jamie?" Rachel said. "What are you doing?"

Jamie folded her arms on her stomach.

"Looking at pictures," she mumbled.

Rachel sat down next to her and picked up the pictures.

"I miss our old room," she said.

"Me, too," Jamie said. "I miss everything."

"I wish Spotsey was here, at least," Rachel said.

Jamie nodded. The night he'd died they had buried him right away. She'd hoped they could move his grave to their new house, but it had taken a few days to get everything settled, and by that time, Mrs. Harrison had told her, he was better off staying where he was.

"Maybe we could put a grave marker in our yard for Spotsey," Jamie said. "Sort of like a gravestone, so we can remember him."

"Yeah," said Rachel. "We never got to have a very good funeral."

Jamie got out her pens and a small square of paper. She drew a yellow and green pattern around the edges. Then she picked up the blue pen and wrote:

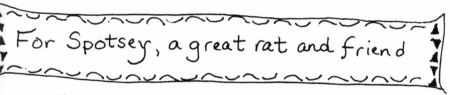

For Spotsey, a great rat and friend

She put on her shoes.

"Can I come?" Rachel asked.

"Yeah," Jamie said. "Get Mom and Dad, too."

Then she remembered Sheila. Sheila could have written a really good poem for the marker. She'd probably have started crying right away at the funeral, so Jamie wouldn't have to be the first one.

Jamie met Rachel and their parents in the kitchen. She led them out to the backyard. She was already thinking of the right place.

The yard was small and empty, with one little tree in the middle. Bushes grew around its edges, stopping at the back wall. Jamie went to a corner of the wall, and knelt down by a patch of dirt.

"Are you sure you want this spot?" her dad asked. "You can put it near the flowers by the side of the house, if you'd like."

"I'm sure," she said. She dug her marker into the ground.

"Let's say a prayer," Rachel said.

"How about you say a prayer in your head," Jamie said.

Rachel shrugged, but she closed her eyes.

Jamie's mom put her arm around Jamie's shoulders and squeezed her.

Jamie pictured Spotsey. *I miss you,* she told him.

She opened her eyes. Then she let her parents walk ahead so that she could get a last look.

"I've never seen anybody care so much for a rat," her dad was saying to her mom.

"Spotsey wasn't a normal rat," her mom said. "He went outside, he ran around the room. She played with him the way other kids play with their dogs."

Jamie stared at the dirt. *You were better than a dog,* she told Spotsey. Then she turned around and walked through the dry grass toward the back door, taking a last look at the gravestone. It was a pretty good funeral, really. The only thing missing was Sheila. Jamie headed into her room and opened her backpack. It was time to write Sheila a letter.

Chapter Four

Jamie rubbed her shoes back and forth on the smooth floor under her desk, listening to Mrs. Hazelett.

"I have a list here of your reading groups," Mrs. Hazelett was saying. "When I call your name, come get your book."

Jamie watched the kids go up one by one. Mrs. Hazelett handed out purple books, then red books, and finally green books. Jamie glanced over at the book in front of Elise. She had never seen it before. In fact, all of the reading books looked strange. At her old school, she had been looking forward to her next book, *Bridges,* with a bridge leading to an island on the cover.

Jamie felt the quiet of the room. She glanced up.

"I'll ask once more just to make sure," Mrs. Hazelett said. "Is there anyone who didn't get a book?"

Jamie raised her hand.

"Jamie," Mrs. Hazelett nodded. "I almost forgot. We need to find out which reading group you belong in."

She took a piece of paper out of her desk.

"Here," she said, leaning close to Jamie. "You can read this story and then answer the questions at the bottom of the page."

Jamie looked carefully at the paper in front of her.

"The rest of us are going to be reading to ourselves, so it shouldn't be too noisy for you," Mrs. Hazelett added.

"Is this all I need?" Jamie asked.

"Yes," Mrs. Hazelett smiled. "Just your eyes and your pencil."

Your pencil. Jamie felt the backs of her legs sticking to her chair. She managed to nod at Mrs. Hazelett, who was taking forever to turn back around.

Jamie looked at the kids around her out of the corner of her eye. Everyone had a pencil. Some people had their own paper. How could she not have noticed?

At her old school, her teacher had a pencil box with thirty-two pencils inside. She passed them out in the morning, and collected them at the end of the day. Only kids who forgot to return the pencils two times in a row had to bring their own. Then again, at her old school, she wouldn't have minded walking up to the front of the room and asking to borrow something she forgot to bring.

Jamie looked up. Mrs. Hazelett was talking softly to the class, so softly she was impossible to interrupt. Jamie looked down at her paper, but she couldn't keep her eyes on it long enough to read the first sentence. She kept thinking about yesterday, when she came in late. Then she hadn't been able to do the math problem on the board when it was her turn. She closed her eyes. Maybe she could just slip out of the room and start all over again. Only this time, maybe someone could warn her about a few things.

Jamie felt something bump her shoulder. She opened her eyes. Elise nodded toward Jamie's lap as she looked straight at her reader, pretending to follow the story. Jamie looked down. Elise was holding a pencil out under the table.

"Thanks," Jamie whispered, as Elise slipped the pencil into her hand.

"Sure," Elise whispered back. "You better hurry."

Jamie sat between Stephanie and Tanya on the grass, watching the four-square game. She pulled her knees to her chest, lifting her legs off the grass. The wind blew under her legs, mixing with the sweat on the backs of her knees to cool her off. In the distance she spotted Rachel walking toward the bars with some girls from her class. They looked like the girls Jamie had seen by the bus the other day waiting with Rachel in line. As they got nearer to the bars, they began to run, racing to be the first to climb up. Jamie saw Rachel climb to the highest bar and do a flip.

"I'm hot," Stephanie said.

"I wish it was still summer," Tanya said. "I'd go swimming and stay in the pool all day."

"Me, too," said Jamie.

"My mom never lets me swim all day," said Stephanie. "She says I'll get sunburned."

Jamie looked down at her knees. She felt sunburned just from the last ten minutes.

"You get sunburned no matter what," Tanya told Stephanie.

Jamie watched the kids playing four-square. A short girl with a yellow ribbon in her hair was yelling at the boy next to her, and he was yelling back while the other kids watched. None of them looked like they felt too hot to play.

"Maybe we should play four-square," Jamie said.

Stephanie looked at Jamie, her mouth in a line the way it had been when Jamie asked her about washing hands.

"Are you kidding?" she said. "I can't play four-square in

sandals. And you really can't—since you wear socks with yours."

Stephanie said "socks" like they were something she'd never heard of. Jamie looked down at her feet. They looked fine to her.

"Besides," Tanya said. "We have to play four-square in P.E. already. It's boring."

Jamie wanted to ask Tanya if she thought sitting in the shade was exciting, but she decided against it.

"I remember once in P.E., we played and I got hit in the head," Stephanie said, her voice back to normal.

"I remember that." Tanya nodded. "We all stopped playing."

Jamie lay back in the grass. Something about their voices made her tired. She looked for shapes in the tree leaves above her head. She could make out a large fish and a pair of wings. The leaf-wings rustled back and forth, like they were really flying. Jamie squinted at them.

Jamie turned onto her stomach and looked behind her, studying the tree's branches. She saw two pairs of legs dangling from the bottom branches, swinging back and forth. She had never seen the legs wearing purple shorts, but the legs in red shorts looked familiar. As she looked at them more closely, she was reminded of reading class and her pencil.

"What are you looking at?" Stephanie asked her.

"Just some kids playing." Jamie rolled over and sat up.

Stephanie glanced back over her shoulder.

"Where?" she asked. "I don't see any."

"Don't worry," Jamie told her. "It's nothing you'd want to play."

"Anyway," Tanya said. "I was in the middle of my story."

"So?" Stephanie said crossly. "I know this story by heart."

"Well, Jamie doesn't," Tanya said. "Come on, you can tell parts of it, too."

Stephanie shrugged.

Jamie tried to listen to Tanya. Her voice reminded Jamie of the trains that ran behind her grandparents' house, making the same sound for so long that Jamie stopped hearing it after a while. She nodded like she was listening, and secretly glanced at the branches above her. The legs disappeared, making the leaves shake behind them. Jamie was sure they must be climbing toward the top. She turned back to the rush of Tanya's voice, waiting for the shrill whistle that would bring it to a stop and call them all back to class.

Chapter Five

Jamie kicked a dried-up lemon along the sidewalk, passing it to Rachel as they headed home from the bus.

"Jamie." Rachel looked over at her. "How come you always lie in the grass during recess? Are you sick or something?"

"I might as well be," Jamie said. "The nurse's office is probably more exciting than recess anyway." She shook her head. "At our old school, recess was the best part of the day."

Rachel kicked the lemon back toward Jamie.

"I still think it's the best part," Rachel said. "And this playground even has two sets of swings, and tetherballs, and two sets of bars. I'm teaching everybody how to do flips."

"You're lucky," Jamie said. "In my class, there's nobody who'd want to learn how to flip. All the girls want to do is lie in the grass."

"I don't ever want to go to fourth grade here," said Rachel. "I wish you could just play with us."

Jamie rolled her eyes. She could see it now: she'd be running around the playground with a group of girls Rachel's age. Stephanie and Tanya would tell everyone in her class that she played with second graders, and she could forget about making friends her own age.

"At least we can play now," Jamie told Rachel.

"What do you want to do?" Rachel asked.

Jamie tried to remember a game that she liked. It felt too hot to ride bikes, and there were no other kids outside to start hide-and-seek. Then she thought of something that would work in Phoenix.

"Let's spy," she said. "We haven't done that since we've been here."

"We better be careful," Rachel said. "Last time we got caught by Mr. Booth he chased us three blocks. And after he called Mom, she almost grounded us for a month."

"But that's why it's perfect," Jamie said. "No one knows us here, and no one knows Mom. We're practically invisible."

Rachel smiled. She kicked the lemon back and forth between her feet, keeping it away from Jamie while she thought it over. Jamie reached her foot over to take it back, and Rachel kicked the lemon sideways, making it fly into the yard next to them.

"Great," said Jamie.

Rachel peered over to where the lemon landed. As she picked it up, she crouched down on her knees.

"What are you doing?" Jamie asked.

"Sh!" Rachel whispered. "I think I just found our first place to spy."

Jamie looked at the house in the middle of the yard. Its blinds were shut, like most of the houses in Phoenix, which made Jamie nervous. She hated wondering whether some-one inside could see out.

"I don't know." She turned to Rachel. But Rachel was al-ready dashing across the grass to the side of the house. Jamie ran to catch up with her, trying to hop lightly and leave the grass without making footprints.

"Look," Rachel whispered. She stepped back, and Jamie followed her gaze. The thick oleander bushes spread between the house and its next-door neighbor, reaching almost as high as the houses themselves. They parted slightly where Rachel stood, and Jamie could see a thin path winding through the middle of the dark green leaves, hidden to any-one on either side.

"Should we try it?" Rachel asked.

Jamie looked around. The street was still empty.

"Okay," she said. "But we have to remember the way back."

"You first," Rachel said.

Jamie stepped forward. Sometimes she wished they had another sister who was the oldest, and Jamie could make her go first. She took careful steps, with Rachel close behind her. The path was perfect to sneak through, since its bushes were thick above their heads, but had no leaves near the ground. Jamie felt that she was in a cool, green tunnel. She followed the tunnel until she could see a patch of bright light streaming out in front of them. She stopped quickly, and Rachel bumped into her, landing on Jamie's right heel.

"Ow!" she hissed.

"You shouldn't stop so fast," Rachel whispered. She peered past Jamie. "Where are we?"

"I don't know," Jamie said. "But we're at the end of the tunnel."

She got down on her hands and knees, and peeked around the corner of the bushes. At first, the light jumped in her way, but soon she could see hundreds of red and yellow flowers. The flowers surrounded a circle of grass which was just big enough for the white metal table and chair that sat at its center. They spread back to the edges of the yard, reaching up around the trunks of the yard's trees. The trees were six tall islands growing up from the flowers: two with palm leaves, and four with long branches that loomed over the yard, covering it in shadows. Along the back of the yard, and on each side, oleander bushes grew with their white flowers, stretching so high that it was impossible to see anything outside the garden. The back wall of the house was covered in ivy, making even the fourth side of the garden completely green.

"Wow," said Jamie under her breath.

"What is it?" Rachel asked.

Jamie scooted over to let Rachel see.

"It's like a different world," Rachel said.

Jamie stared at the sea of yellow and red, dark green and white. She felt like she was miles away from Phoenix, with its flat open yards full of brown grass. The flowers here belonged in a jungle or somewhere she'd never been. She wanted to run into the middle of the garden and be completely surrounded by them. She leaned forward to get a better look.

"Jamie!" Rachel put her arms out to hold Jamie back. "Look!"

The ivy on the house separated as the door beneath it

opened. A woman in a straw hat moved slowly through the flowers, toward the circle of grass. She didn't look down, but she still avoided every single flower as she stepped, almost as if she floated an inch above them. Jamie thought the woman was going to sit in the white chair, but instead she lowered herself unsteadily to her knees and sat at the edge of the grass.

"What's she doing?" Rachel asked.

"I don't know," Jamie said. "Maybe—"

The woman lifted her head suddenly and looked around her. Jamie tried to pretend she was a rock, and let her breath out as quietly as she could.

The woman picked up a red-handled spade and slowly began to dig. Jamie wondered if she was going to dig her way around the garden and end up by their passageway. She pictured the woman looking up to see two sets of eyes peering through the oleanders. She'd probably have a heart attack.

"Jamie," Rachel tugged at her shirt. "Mom's gonna wonder where we are."

Jamie nodded. She stood up slowly, watching the woman's back through the bushes. Carefully, Jamie turned around. Rachel tiptoed in front of her, and they crept along the path until they reached the opening. When the coast was clear, they ran across the front yard to the sidewalk.

"Wow," said Rachel. "Our first time spying, and we already found a secret passage."

Jamie had almost forgotten the passage. She was busy thinking about the woman who knelt by the flowers.

"And a person to spy on," she said. "We need to think up a code name for her."

"I thought of one already," Rachel said. "How about Miss Opal?"

Jamie looked over at Rachel. She had to admit, it was a pretty good name.

"Do you think Miss Opal lives in that house alone?" she asked Rachel.

"Maybe," Rachel answered.

Jamie shuddered. The house looked too big for one person, and dark with the shades drawn.

"Maybe she's a grandmother," she said. "And her grandkids live with her."

"The house was too quiet," Rachel said. "And besides, the flowers were all over, and none of them were stepped on."

Jamie nodded. For some reason, she didn't mind thinking of the woman alone in the flowers. It was only imagining her in the house that bothered her.

"What was she digging?" Rachel asked.

"I don't know," said Jamie. "But she never took her eyes off it."

"Yeah," said Rachel. "She looked like she was in a trance."

Jamie wished they could go back right now and interrupt the trance to ask her what she was doing. But what if she turned around suddenly and gave them a creepy smile? Or what if she grabbed them for sneaking around? They would be stuck, surrounded by the red and yellow flowers, with no one to hear them yell for help.

"Jamie." Rachel's voice pushed the evil smile away. "I said, what do you think?"

"About what?"

"Will she chase us out if she sees us?"

Jamie pictured the woman bending over the flowers.

"I don't know. I didn't get to see her face," Jamie said. "But she doesn't look very fast."

"Grandma doesn't look fast either," Rachel said. "And you know how fast she is when she's mad. Remember the time we were spying at her house, and we fell out of the broom closet right next to her?"

Jamie smiled.

"Yeah. And even when Grandma's not fast, her voice can freeze you so you can't run away at all."

"I'd hate to be frozen in that garden," Rachel said.

Jamie pictured herself standing in the passageway as the woman came closer and closer. Suddenly, her feet would be stuck to the ground no matter how hard she tried to lift them.

"We'll just have to be careful."

Rachel nodded. She pulled the lemon out of her pocket and kicked it right to Jamie. They passed it between them as they made their way home.

Chapter Six

Jamie finished her math problems and turned her paper over. She shielded a corner with one hand. In the corner, she drew two squirrels like the ones that lived by her old house.

"Okay," Mrs. Hazelett said. "Everyone looks ready to me."

She handed out colored pencils.

"Now, switch papers with the person next to you, and get ready to grade."

Jamie turned her paper back over and handed it to Elise. She looked down at Elise's paper. The numbers were sort of messy, and all of the twos were made into snakes.

The class began to read the problems out loud. Jamie graded them one by one, trying hard to pay attention long enough to hear the answers. Soon they switched papers back. Elise had marked four of Jamie's answers wrong.

"Take a look at your papers and we'll try to figure out the mistakes," Mrs. Hazelett said.

Jamie wasn't too interested in her mistakes. She turned her paper over. She was about to draw on the top corner when she noticed something new near her squirrels. At their feet, she saw words so messy they could have been blades of grass or part of the ground. She looked closely.

She glanced over at Elise, who was trying to figure out her math mistakes. Jamie tore a small corner off her spelling practice sheet. In small letters, she wrote her answer. She slipped the corner onto Elise's desk. Elise bent down to study the message.

Out of the corner of her eye, Jamie watched her read the tiny yes.

Jamie studied the crust of her cold grilled-cheese sandwich. She glanced at the other kids. Everyone was almost finished eating, except Stephanie, who was in the middle of telling a story. Jamie looked over at Elise. Elise raised her eyebrows, and Jamie nodded. They slipped out the cafeteria door, leaving Stephanie an only slightly smaller audience.

"The other class is already out here," Elise said.

Jamie noticed a short girl with long black hair running toward them from behind. Before she could say anything, the girl snuck up behind Elise and jumped on her back.

"I was just looking for you," Elise said, quickly twisting herself so the girl didn't have a chance of staying on.

The girl unwrapped her arms from around Elise.

"No fair," she said. "You're so much taller you barely have to try to get free."

"Tara, this is Jamie," Elise said.

Tara turned to Jamie, as if she'd just appeared out of nowhere.

"Hi," Jamie said.

"Hi." Tara smiled. "Are you the one who forgot your pencil?"

Jamie looked at Tara's knees. They were covered with dirt.

"Yeah," Jamie said. "That was me, all right."

"Hey, don't be embarrassed," Tara said. "I forget mine all the time."

"It's not that," Jamie told her. "I didn't even know I had to bring one."

"She's new," Elise said to Tara.

Tara looked at Jamie.

"What does being new have to do with bringing a pencil?" she asked.

Jamie looked at Tara. She wondered if Tara had ever been new before.

"Things are different here," Jamie said.

Tara's mouth opened slightly, and then she caught Elise's eye. She nodded.

"Come on," Elise said. "Let's go to the tree."

Jamie walked between the two friends.

"Wait till you see it," Tara told her.

They reached the trunk of the biggest tree in the school yard. Jamie ran her fingers across the bark. It was smooth, with thin, dark lines running up it. The bottom branches began above her shoulder and stretched out far over the grass.

Elise locked her hands together and held them low for Tara to step on. Tara climbed up. She stood on the lowest branch for a second, then reached up to climb higher.

"Want a boost?" Elise said. "I mean, 'cause you're short, like Tara."

"Okay," Jamie said.

She grabbed the branch and stood for a second on Elise's hands. She pulled her knee up to the branch she was holding and moved her hands to the next branch above her. Soon she could see Tara.

The three of them moved through the leaves.

"Here," Tara said, peering down at Jamie. "Scoot out on this one."

Jamie climbed up and moved out the branch until it was almost too skinny to hold her. She rested her feet on the branch below, watching Tara and Elise move to places nearby.

"It's great up here when the irrigation comes," Tara said.

"Irrigation?" Jamie asked, settling onto her branch.

"Yeah," Tara said. "Once a month all the yards get flooded to water the grass. They usually do it at night, but sometimes it happens during school. Then you can sit up here and watch all the frogs and crawdads swimming around in the water."

"Wow," Jamie said. "I hope it happens soon."

Elise sat carefully on one branch and hooked her feet under another lower down. She leaned back in a back bend and let her arms dangle below. Tara followed, and finally Jamie hooked her own feet and leaned back.

Jamie opened her eyes. The entire playground was upside down, and the tiny kids below her looked like they were hanging from their feet on a giant dirt ceiling.

Tara swung her arms back and forth.

"Look," she said. "The shadow looks like a shark moving on the grass."

Jamie peered straight down through the leaves to see Stephanie and Tanya sitting below, probably fighting over whose turn it was to talk. In the distance, she could see Rachel and the second-grade girls swinging on the bars. Jamie let go with her hands, and her arms hung free, swinging back and forth above the grass.

"Your shadow looks like two ribbons," Tara told her. "Or maybe one big bird with long wings."

Jamie waved her arms faster.

"Yeah," she said. She watched her bird fly below her. From up here, she could see what Rachel meant about the playground. Kids were running everywhere, while she swung above them. And for the first time, she noticed, the playground grass looked green.

Chapter Seven

Jamie couldn't fall asleep. Every time she shut her eyes, she heard Stephanie and Tanya. They weren't so bad when they told stories, but when they asked questions Jamie couldn't stand it. What was wrong with wearing socks and sandals, anyway? She sat up.

"Which one?" Rachel mumbled above her.

"What?" Jamie asked.

"Which one are you going to choose?"

Jamie rolled over.

"Rachel, I'm trying to go to sleep."

Rachel jumped off her bunk and sat down on Jamie's bed. Jamie sat up and rubbed her eyes, peering closely at Rachel. Rachel's face had a look Jamie had never seen before. Her eyes focused on something far away from Jamie, making her look distracted, almost vacant.

"Come on," she said to Jamie. "Just tell me which one you're choosing."

"Choosing for what?" Jamie asked her, still trying to catch Rachel's eye.

Rachel got up from the bed and began to pace back and forth. Something about the way she walked made Jamie afraid to tell her to stop.

"You know," Rachel said impatiently. "There's the red team, the yellow team, and the blue team. It's time to pick."

Jamie shook her head.

"Pick for what?"

Rachel folded her arms across her chest.

"You have to," she insisted, ignoring Jamie's question. "And Angie says to hurry up."

"Who's Angie?" Jamie asked. But Rachel just kept pacing.

Jamie stood up.

"If I pick, will you go back to bed? It's the middle of the night."

"I kind of wanted to play," Rachel said.

"We can play when we wake up," Jamie told her. "Can't we wait till then?"

"All right," Rachel said. "But that's only if you pick."

"Fine," Jamie said. "I'll take the red one."

Rachel shook her head.

"I hope that's the right team," she said. "It'll be hard to switch."

"I'll think about it tomorrow," Jamie said.

"I can't hear you," Rachel said loudly.

"Ssh—Mom and Dad are asleep," Jamie said. "It's practically two in the morning."

Jamie crawled back under her covers as Rachel climbed up to her bunk. She hoped she'd picked the right team. Then again, she didn't even know what kind of team it was. She would have to wait till the morning to figure it out. She didn't want to think about it now. Jamie watched Rachel's mattress wires move up and down as she eased herself to sleep. Soon Rachel was snoring. Jamie closed her eyes. She needed all the sleep she could get.

Jamie could hear Rachel in the kitchen. She pushed her sheet off and sorted through her clothes. She picked out her purple shorts and white T-shirt. She could already hear Stephanie asking if everyone in Colorado wore white T-shirts. She felt like putting on her dad's shirt and shorts. That would give Stephanie something to frown about. If Sheila were here, she'd probably get Jamie to do it, so they could laugh about it later.

Jamie went into the kitchen. Her mom and Rachel sat at the table, eating cereal. Her dad looked up from pouring his coffee.

"Hi, Jamie," he said. "You slept a long time."

"I couldn't fall asleep."

"Why not?" her dad asked.

"Well, first I was thinking, and then Rachel started talking to me."

"What do you mean?" Rachel looked up from her cereal.

"You know," Jamie told her. "About the teams."

"Teams?" Rachel stared at her.

"Come on," said Jamie. "You wanted me to choose a team, and you wouldn't go to sleep until I said I would."

"Are you sure?" Rachel asked,

Jamie looked at her. She always knew when Rachel was lying, and this wasn't one of those times.

"What did I say?"

"You said I needed to pick between the red, yellow, and blue teams. You sat down on my bed, and then you started walking around the room while you told me about it. You said I had to hurry and pick soon." As Jamie told the story, it started to make less sense.

Rachel laughed.

"No I didn't."

"You did, I promise," Jamie said. "I couldn't think that up on my own."

"But what were the teams for?" Rachel asked.

"I don't know," Jamie said. "That's what I wanted to ask you."

"You must have been sleepwalking," their mom said, looking up from her breakfast at Rachel.

Rachel looked at Jamie, turning her spoon back and forth between her thumb and finger.

"That's weird," Jamie said. "I've never seen you sleepwalk before. I've never really seen anyone sleepwalk before."

"Have you ever sleepwalked?" Rachel asked her mom.

"No, but your dad talks in his sleep."

Their dad came over to the table.

"I walked in my sleep growing up, too," he said. "Whenever something was making me tense."

"Am I tense?" Rachel asked.

"You don't look tense," he said. He glanced at their mom. Jamie looked at Rachel.

"But what about choosing teams?" she asked.

"I don't know," Rachel said.

Jamie glanced at her dad, but he was looking at Rachel.

"We better go," Jamie said, gulping down her orange juice. "We're going to miss the bus."

Chapter Eight

Jamie and Rachel stood at the corner waiting for the bus to pull away before they crossed the street. Jamie watched three girls from Rachel's class wave from the back window of the bus. As Rachel waved back, one girl pushed the other two aside, and took up the entire window with her wave. Rachel put her hands in her pockets.

"Is that Angie?" Jamie asked.

Rachel frowned at her.

"How did you know?" she said.

Jamie looked at Rachel. She walked evenly, her arms folded across her chest.

"I guess she looks like an Angie," she lied.

"She's Angie all right," Rachel muttered.

"Is she one of the girls you play with at recess?"

Rachel nodded.

"I thought you liked playing with them," Jamie said. She almost reminded Rachel that she'd said recess was better here than at their old school, but she decided against it.

"I used to," Rachel said.

Jamie looked at the bus in the distance. She grabbed Rachel's shoulder and looked at her closely.

"What happened? Did Angie do something to you?"

She looked past Rachel, to recess tomorrow. She'd come over to the second graders, and Angie would be sorry. Maybe Elise and Tara would come with her. That would make Angie think again before she pushed somebody out of the way, especially if that somebody happened to be Rachel.

"Not to me," Rachel said.

Jamie let go of her shoulder.

"She just tries to get me on her side all the time," Rachel said. "Three of the girls are in this big fight and they all want me on their side. Since I'm new, I'm the only one who hasn't taken a side. They all try to get me to choose between them. In class we pick partners during reading every day, and so I have to pick one of them. As soon as I do, the other two are mean to me for the rest of the day."

"Well, who do you like most, of the three of them?"

Rachel shook her head. "I don't like any of them, really. And I wouldn't care, except that all the other girls are on sides too, so if I don't pick one, there's no one to play with."

"They all took sides?" Jamie shook her head. "Maybe you should climb the tree with me and Elise and Tara."

"Maybe," Rachel said. But she didn't look very convinced.

"Or maybe the fight will end soon."

"Maybe," Rachel said. Jamie watched her begin to walk a little faster, and then slow down suddenly.

"Hey, Jamie," she said. "I know what we can do today."

"What?" Jamie asked.

Rachel nodded her head toward the house with the oleander passageway.

"Okay," Jamie said. "Maybe we can see what she was digging up, this time."

Rachel insisted on leading the way, even though she looked scared. Jamie followed close behind. She watched the ground in front of her, stepping only on dirt and moving around the small sticks that might crack under her shoes. She stopped close to Rachel at the edge of the opening.

"Jamie," Rachel hissed. "She's digging again."

Jamie sat down and peered through the bottom branches of the oleanders. The woman sat at the edge of the grass, digging with her red spade. Her arms moved more quickly than they had the last time, and she hit the dirt hard with each stroke.

"Let's see if we can get closer," Rachel said. Just as she rose from her knees, Jamie saw the wall of ivy split apart. The door behind it swung open.

"Stay still!" Jamie whispered.

A tall woman with black hair hurried out into the yard.

"What are you doing?" the woman asked Miss Opal, sticking her black sandal right in front of the red spade.

"Be careful of the flowers," Miss Opal said.

"Be careful? Be careful?" The tall woman shook her head and tapped her foot. As she tapped, her head began to shake faster, in rhythm with her toes. "I couldn't care less about the flowers!"

Jamie glanced at Rachel, who stared back at her.

Miss Opal put her spade down on the grass. She turned to look up at the woman, and the woman unfolded her arms from across her chest.

"Really," Miss Opal said, sweeping her arm across the flowers toward the trees. "I'm fine out here."

Jamie leaned forward. The tall woman seemed to be shrinking.

"It's not your being out here that worries me," the woman said. She picked up the spade. "I really don't think you should be working."

Rachel nudged Jamie.

"Why can't she work?" she whispered.

Jamie shrugged her shoulders. She looked back at the two women just in time to catch Miss Opal glancing in her direction.

Miss Opal laughed.

"You know, I'm glad you didn't visit me when I lived in India or Turkey. We spent all day building, gardening, walking."

The tall woman shook her head.

"That was five years ago," she said. "And you know it's not the same now."

Jamie looked at Rachel.

"Maybe something happened to her," Rachel whispered, keeping her eyes on the two women.

"Don't worry. Just go on inside," Miss Opal was saying, her voice softer now. "I'm almost finished, and then we can go."

The tall woman shook her head again, but she handed Miss Opal the spade and slipped back through the door.

Miss Opal picked up her spade and began digging.

"I don't suppose you're going to come out," she said, studying the ground in front of her.

Jamie peered as far as she could, to see what refused to leave the ground.

"What's she talking to?" Rachel whispered.

"You must know I can see your feet," Miss Opal continued.

Jamie gulped. Rachel stiffened next to her.

"I don't necessarily mind visitors, but I like to know who they are."

Rachel rose to her feet. Jamie got ready to run back along the path, but Rachel moved toward the flowers. Jamie sighed. Slowly, she followed Rachel through the path to the garden.

Miss Opal stood up as they walked toward her. Jamie stepped with her eyes on the ground, trying not to crush any flowers.

"We were just, umm, we just saw the path," Rachel said.

"We're sorry," Jamie added. "We shouldn't have come in your yard. We know it's trespassing."

She looked up at Miss Opal. Her eyes were blue and gray at the same time, reminding Jamie of a rocky stream.

"Well," Miss Opal said, "you're lucky I'm the one you ran into." She motioned toward the door. "Laura might have chased you all the way home."

"We don't mean to bother you," Jamie said.

"What are your names?" Miss Opal asked.

"I'm Jamie," Jamie said. "And this is Rachel." She looked

over at Rachel, who wasn't paying any attention. Instead she was kneeling by the flowers.

"Rachel!" Jamie said.

"Sorry. I was just looking at them." Rachel scowled at Jamie.

"Aren't they pretty?" Miss Opal said.

Rachel nodded. "They're beautiful. I've never seen flowers like them before."

"Never?" Miss Opal asked.

"We've never seen anything like this whole garden before," Jamie said. She wondered if Miss Opal knew that she probably had the only one in Phoenix.

"That's why we came back," Rachel said.

Jamie rolled her eyes.

"Don't worry," Miss Opal said to Jamie. "I saw you last time, too. I almost invited you to come sit with me, but you ran away."

Jamie studied the flowers by her feet.

"Do you live nearby?" Miss Opal asked.

"We live around the corner," Rachel said. "For now at least. But our real home is in Colorado. We just left there. We might go back in a year."

"I've only visited Colorado. But I thought it was a beautiful place," Miss Opal said.

"It is," Jamie said.

"It must be hard to leave your home behind," Miss Opal said. She looked at Jamie, catching her in the gray of her eyes. It seemed like she could have been one of Jamie's grandma's friends, who all remembered Jamie as a baby and hugged her whenever they saw her.

"You must miss it very much."

Jamie nodded. Suddenly she felt like she had a thousand things to tell Miss Opal and she didn't know where to start. She was thinking of how to begin when Laura's voice interrupted her.

"We need to hurry!" she called out from the house.

Miss Opal turned to Jamie and Rachel.

"Well, Jamie and Rachel, my garden has been a second home to many people. I enjoy hearing stories while I work, so I'd be happy to have your company if you'd like to visit."

"Really?" Rachel asked.

Miss Opal looked from her to Jamie. "Really," she said, patting their shoulders before she turned and moved smoothly through the doorway into the cool, dark house.

The door shut behind Miss Opal, and Jamie watched the ivy form one long wall again.

Rachel tugged at Jamie's elbow.

"Why did she have to go with that woman?" she asked.

Jamie had forgotten about the tall woman—Laura, Miss Opal had called her—who was waiting behind the ivy wall.

"I don't know, but it must have been important," Jamie said. "Laura was sure in a big hurry."

Rachel shook her head.

"Remember how she said, 'Be careful? Be careful?'" Rachel's eyes bulged out, imitating Laura.

"Yeah," Jamie said. "She almost exploded."

"I'd be scared to go anywhere with her," Rachel said.

Jamie hoped Miss Opal didn't feel like that. But she hadn't looked scared. Then again, she hadn't looked very excited either.

"I wonder where they're going," Jamie said.

"I don't know," Rachel said. "Maybe you could ask her next time."

"Maybe," Jamie said. She peered at the ivy wall. Then she turned in a circle, looking at the garden. It was beginning to feel too quiet.

"Come on," she told Rachel. "Let's go home."

Chapter Nine

Jamie sat on the gym floor between Elise and Stephanie, waiting for Mr. Bixbie to tell them what they were going to play next. He paced back and forth, listening for silence. He reminded Jamie of a hungry fish in a bowl circling for food. When the class got as quiet as it was going to get, he stopped moving.

"Okay," he said finally. "It's Friday and you've run hard today, so I'm going to give you free time for the rest of the period."

The class couldn't be quiet about that.

"Hold on," he said. "You have to decide on a game. Who has a suggestion?"

"Let's play crab soccer," Paul offered.

Jamie liked that game. She was pretty good at walking

backwards on her hands and feet, and she never fell when she kicked the ball.

"Any other suggestions?" Mr. Bixbie asked.

"TV tag!" yelled Stephanie.

The class started to yell with her.

"Well, Stephanie," Mr. Bixbie said, "it looks like the class likes your idea."

Jamie tried as fast as she could to think of a better game. But the class was already voting and TV tag was sure to win. If it had come up at the beginning of class she could have pretended to be sick.

Jamie tried to listen to Mr. Bixbie explain the rules, but she was starting to feel hot. The rules weren't the problem. She knew she had to name a different TV show each time she got tagged so she'd be freed. The problem was the shows. Jamie was used to not being allowed to watch much TV, but she wasn't used to explaining it to other kids. No one had bothered her at her old school, but here it might be different.

"Okay," Mr. Bixbie said, "Stephanie will be it. When I blow the whistle, the game begins."

"Elise!" Jamie whispered.

Elise looked up from tying her shoe.

"Can you tell me some shows?"

Elise raised her eyebrows, but she started to name shows.

"On your mark, get set . . ."

"Thanks," Jamie whispered. She repeated the shows in her head as she ran across the gym, racing away from Stephanie. Luckily, as she'd guessed, Stephanie was slow. But just as Jamie stopped to catch her breath, Stephanie leaped out of nowhere, tagging her shoulder.

"Name a show," she said.

Jamie couldn't remember exactly what Elise had said. She could guess, but what if the name came out wrong?

"Come on," Stephanie said, looking around for other kids to tag. "Or you'll stay frozen."

Jamie felt a tap on the back.

"*Rescue Squad,*" Elise whispered into her ear. Then, before Stephanie could tag her, she ran to the other side of the room.

"*Rescue Squad,*" Jamie said to Stephanie.

"You're free," Stephanie said, and ran to tag someone else.

The whistle blew to end the game, and Jamie stumbled back to her spot on the gym floor. She was safe for now, but she knew she'd have to learn some shows before next Friday's gym class.

She sat down next to Elise, trying to breathe softer.

Stephanie slowed down as she walked past them.

"I know you two cheated," she whispered. "How come you didn't know a show?"

Jamie looked at Stephanie. If she told her about not watching much TV, Jamie would never hear the end of it. Stephanie was bothered enough by her socks.

"Who cares?" Elise said. "I watch you cheat in spelling all the time. Do I come up and ask you about knowing the words?"

Stephanie rolled her eyes.

"I still think it's weird," she said, marching back to her seat.

Elise sat calmly, tapping her fingers on the gym floor.

The class settled down on the floor. They were supposed to be closing their eyes and relaxing, but it was too hot to relax all the way.

"Thanks," Jamie whispered. "We've never had a TV till now. My parents don't let us watch very much."

Elise nodded.

"My cousins are like that," she said. "Then when they come over to our house, all they want to do is watch TV."

"Do you get to watch as much as you want?" Jamie asked.

"Yeah," Elise said. "But I don't really like watching alone. My brother and sister are too little to watch my shows. They'd rather hear stories."

"How little are they?" Jamie asked.

"Three and four," Elise said. She tucked her knees up to her chest.

Jamie pictured a boy and a girl like Elise, both tiny, running around and asking for stories.

"I bet your mom and dad get tired of reading," Jamie said.

"I'm the one who gets tired," Elise said. "My parents never really read to them. I've been doing it for a while, though. I read to them every night, but only one story each. Otherwise I'd go crazy."

"Yeah," Jamie said.

"Girls." Mr. Bixbie paced toward them. "This is relaxation time."

Mr. Bixbie looked like he needed his own relaxation time. Jamie rolled her eyes at Elise and then lay on her stomach, using her arms for a pillow. She closed her eyes and pictured putting her head inside of her freezer, letting all the ice cubes fall on top of it.

"Kids," Mr. Bixbie said. "I have one more announcement. As you know, Track and Field Day is coming up soon. The only event you need to sign up for is the three-legged race. If you want to be in it, find a partner and let me know during gym on Monday."

Jamie rolled over on her side. At her old school, the three-legged race was her favorite event. In fact, it seemed like it was everybody's favorite. People chose partners at the beginning of the year so they could start practicing. She wondered if Sheila had a partner this year. Last year, they'd practiced almost every day together until they were so fast they were like one person running alone. They'd won the race for the whole third grade.

Jamie opened her eyes. Elise was facing her, tapping her fingers on the floor.

"Elise?" Jamie said. "Have you ever done the three-legged race?"

"I did in second grade, but not last year," she said.

"Do you want to this year?" Jamie asked. She pulled her arms close to her chest and rested on top of them.

"Okay," she said. "But we need to practice. Believe it or not, Stephanie and Tanya are pretty good. We have to beat them."

Jamie grinned.

"Yeah, it'd be terrible if they won."

She rocked back and forth on her arms. Hopefully, she wouldn't have much homework today. She needed to write Sheila a letter. Sheila was probably planning her own three-legged race by now, and this way they could be thinking about it at the same time. The race made Colorado and Arizona seem closer together. And Jamie didn't care where she raced, as long as she got to run, feel her legs pick up speed and propel her through the dirt to the finish line.

Chapter Ten

Jamie followed Rachel off the bus.

"Do you think we'll ever get used to our new house?" she asked Rachel.

"I like our bunk beds," Rachel said. "I'm almost used to our room. The thing I can't get used to is school."

Jamie kicked the pebbles lying by the curb as she walked. The school had seemed weird at first, but Mrs. Hazelett was getting nicer.

"You mean your teacher or the kids?" Jamie asked.

"The kids," Rachel said. "Mainly the girls. They're still fighting over whose side I'll be on. They fight over everything."

Jamie slowed down to walk beside Rachel.

"What about Sara? You go to her house . . ."

"I like playing at Sara's," Rachel said. "And I guess I like Gina. But I hate it when they're all together."

Jamie remembered sitting between Elise and Stephanie in gym.

"I know what you mean," she said.

Rachel opened the mailbox while Jamie got the front door key out of her lunch box.

"Jamie!" Rachel ran up the sidewalk. "We each got a letter!"

Jamie left the key in the lock. She read the envelope Rachel handed her. The left corner said "S.A.M."

"Who's Sam?" Rachel asked.

"Sheila Ann Margolis," Jamie said. She tore open the envelope. Sheila had sealed the letter with a sticker for privacy. Jamie carefully slit the seal with her finger.

Dear Jamie,
I miss you very very very infinity much!
How is Phoenix? Is it still hot? Is Mrs. Hazlet still weird? I cried when I got your letter about Spotsey. I missed him when you guys left but now I miss him more.

School is boring without you. Beth and I stopped our spy club but we can start it when you come back. Tell your parents you <u>have</u> to — no matter what. You can lie and say I got really sick and you have to see me.
Write back soon! Love, S.A.M.

Jamie looked up. Rachel was still reading her letter. She glanced over Rachel's shoulder.

"Hey!" Rachel covered the letter.

"Who's it from?" Jamie asked.

"Jessica," Rachel said. "She writes sort of messy."

Jamie liked messy writers. She'd gotten Cs in handwriting ever since she started getting grades, and before that it was ✓–. Even when she tried really hard, her teachers complained. So far Mrs. Hazelett hadn't said anything, but the end of the quarter was coming up.

"Boulder sounds fun," Rachel said.

"I know," Jamie said.

Sheila and Beth were probably swinging in the park right now.

"I miss the park," Jamie said.

"Yeah," Rachel said. "I wonder when we'll get to see it again?"

"We might even be back by next summer," Jamie said. She turned the key in the lock, but the door was already open. She could hear music blaring out the living room window. She pictured her mom inside, playing along on an invisible violin. Her mom always liked music to be so loud it surrounded her, so she could be in it even when she wasn't the one playing.

"Jamie? Rachel?" her mom called over the music.

"Hi, Mom," Jamie said. She walked into the kitchen as her mom turned down the stereo.

"Hi, Jamie." Her mom sounded tired, too tired for this early in the afternoon.

"I was just talking to Mrs. Hazelett," she said, looking at Jamie.

"My teacher, Mrs. Hazelett?" Jamie couldn't imagine Mrs. Hazelett and her mom in the same room, much less actually talking to each other.

"Yes," her mom said. "She called to set up our conference. She seems to think we need to have ours as soon as we can."

The tired sound in her mom's voice was beginning to make Jamie nervous.

"When is it?" Jamie asked.

"I told her we could come in Thursday night."

"That's in one week," Rachel said.

"Why does she want it that soon?" Jamie asked.

"She didn't say exactly. But she did say that she'd like you to come with us."

Jamie tried to think of what Mrs. Hazelett would have to say to all of them at once.

"Maybe just you guys should go," she said. "You can tell me what she says."

"I don't think so," her mom said, her voice getting lower. "We'll all go together."

Jamie went to the fridge and got out the orange juice. Maybe her handwriting was so bad that Mrs. Hazelett hadn't been able to read any of her homework, and she'd counted it all wrong.

Jamie slid into the booth and opened Sheila's letter a second time. She was already thinking of what to write back.

"Dear Sheila," she'd begin. "I wish I was back there in class with you."

Jamie felt Mrs. Hazelett standing over her but she couldn't look up. Every time Jamie started to ask her about the conference, Mrs. Hazelett leaned closer, breathing over her shoulder.

"Come on," she hissed. "Come on."

Jamie jolted awake. She was lying in the dark, under her covers. But she could still hear the whispering.

"Come on," Rachel whispered as she jumped off the bed. She walked out of their room, through the kitchen to the back door.

"Where are you going?" Jamie squeezed between Rachel and the door.

"Just come on," Rachel said. "We have to walk home."

Jamie pictured Rachel walking in her sleep through Phoenix until she found Fourteenth Street. Jamie would go with her, and they'd follow Fourteenth Street through the desert, up to the park in Flagstaff, across the four-corner-state lines, through the mountains, and into Boulder. They'd arrive in their nightgowns, shivering in the fall air. The trees on their street would have red leaves by now, and most of the leaves would be scattered on the ground. But their room would be different. Two new girls would be sleeping in their beds.

Jamie looked around their new kitchen. The alley light streaked in the window, hitting the countertop where her parents would soon be making their coffee, where she'd pour her cereal.

"We are home for now," Jamie said.

Rachel smiled sleepily.

"We don't have to walk?"

"We did walk," Jamie said. "Home from the bus, anyway."

"Did we bring everything?" Rachel asked.

Jamie looked at her. She considered trying to understand what Rachel was talking about, but instead she just guessed at what to say to get Rachel back in bed.

"Yup, we brought all of it," Jamie said. "We can go back to bed."

"Okay," Rachel said.

Jamie led her back to their room. She crawled into bed as Rachel climbed up over her head. The bottom bunk welcomed her back.

Chapter Eleven

Jamie and Rachel stood at the edge of Miss Opal's yard.

"Do you think we should knock on the door?" Rachel asked.

Jamie shook her head. "Let's just go through the passageway. She told us to visit her in the garden, remember? And that house is kind of . . . dark."

Rachel nodded. They crossed Miss Opal's yard. In a way, it made Jamie feel proud to walk across it at normal speed instead of sneaking, like she was part of a special club that most people didn't know existed.

"Hello?" Jamie called out as she neared the end of the passageway.

"Hello girls," Miss Opal said, her back to them. As they came closer, Jamie could see that she was still digging.

"Are you planting more flowers?" Rachel asked.

Miss Opal put down her spade and turned around. She caught Jamie's eye, while Jamie settled into the grass next to her, and smiled. Jamie wondered whether she just didn't notice that Jamie sat with slumped shoulders, or if she noticed but didn't care.

"I'll be planting soon," Miss Opal said. "I have to finish weeding first. It always takes longer than you think."

Jamie glanced at the flowers near Miss Opal. One group was completely free from weeds, and it looked like a small island in an ocean of tangled green stems.

"We could help you," Rachel said. "Our mom taught us how. We weeded our whole garden in Colorado."

Jamie looked at the red spade. She had always hated weeding in Colorado, especially when her mom made them weed right after school. But in Miss Opal's garden it looked more interesting.

"I'd love it," Miss Opal said. "Normally I like to do it all myself, but this time I don't seem to be getting very far. I was just wondering whether I could get it all finished."

Jamie wondered why Miss Opal wasn't getting far, but she decided to wait and ask later.

"Do you have any more spades?" she asked instead.

"I have a few old ones," Miss Opal said. She stood up and walked to the side of the house, where she peered into a large bucket. Finally she pulled out two spades along with two sets of wrinkled brown gloves.

Jamie stretched her fingers into her gloves, trying to reach the fingertips. She wiggled her fingers, but the gloves barely came to life.

"I'm sorry," Miss Opal said. "All of my gloves are meant for adults."

"I can just use my bare hands," she told Miss Opal. "If you don't mind."

"Whatever you like," Miss Opal said.

Rachel kept her hands inside her gloves. She picked up her spade and scooted to the edge of the grass.

"Where should I weed, Miss Op—"

Jamie glared at her.

Miss Opal glanced over, but she didn't ask any questions.

"Celia," she said. "And that's a good place to begin, right where you are."

Jamie closed her eyes, trying to make sure "Celia" stayed inside her head. It was hard not to lose track of it, especially now that she and Rachel had said "Miss Opal" so many times.

"Okay, Celia," she said, trying out the name. "Should I start here?"

"Why not?" Celia said. She began to dig again, more smoothly than she had the last time they watched her. But that seemed like years ago, before she'd called them out from the bushes and asked them about missing Colorado.

Celia looked over at Jamie.

"You know, I was just beginning to find out about your move from Colorado when you were here last time. So tell me, when did you come to Phoenix?"

"We came just before school started," Rachel said. "It's not that long ago, but it feels like forever."

Jamie looked over at Rachel. She wondered if Rachel was glad it felt like forever, or if she thought they'd been gone too long already.

"Time really slows down when you're in a new place," Celia said. "Every time I move somewhere new, the first week feels like a month."

Jamie thought back to her first week. The drive itself had felt had like a month, and finding Spotsey stiff in his cage could have been a day alone. And then there was standing outside of the door to Room 408.

Rachel looked at Celia.

"When did you move to Phoenix?" she asked.

"Almost thirty years ago," Celia said. "It's home now. But

since I've been here, I've left and come back a few times. I lived in Turkey for three years, and India for two, I think. And I spent some time in Ohio."

Jamie watched Celia weed.

"Did you want to move?" she asked.

"I did, and I didn't," Celia said. "I loved getting a chance to explore new places and it's just not the same thing when you only go for a visit. When you live somewhere, it grows to be a part of you."

Jamie remembered that Celia had visited Colorado, and she wondered why she didn't want to try living there once she saw it. But it probably looked different if you didn't know anyone around.

"But I don't know," Celia was saying. "I hated to be away from my daughters and my grandchildren. They all stayed in Phoenix, and when I wasn't here, I felt like I was missing a chance, not being with them."

"Is that why you came back?" Jamie asked.

"That was a big part of it," Celia said.

"I know what you mean," Rachel said. "I miss my old friends."

"Do you?" Celia asked.

Rachel nodded.

"I mainly miss Jessica. She was my best friend," Rachel

said. "Here, I probably like Sara the best. I used to like Angie, but not so much anymore."

Jamie glanced over at Celia. Strangely enough, Celia could dig and listen at the same time. Not only was she listening, but she was looking right at Rachel, like she wanted to hear more about it. Then she turned to Jamie.

"How about you?" she asked.

"I miss Sheila," Jamie said. "At first I didn't really like any of the girls here but then I met Elise and her friend Tara. I sit next to Elise in class, which is lucky. But class isn't going so great."

"Oh?" Celia asked.

"She has to have a conference," Rachel explained.

Jamie waited for Celia to turn back into a normal adult and shake her head. Either that or pat her on the hand and say it would all work out in the end. But Celia just continued to look over at Jamie, while she dug into the ground with her spade.

Jamie thought about trying to explain, but as she looked at Celia she realized that she didn't have anything to say, at least anything that was true.

"I can't figure out why we're having it," she said instead. "I just hope it's not something really bad."

"Me too," Rachel said. "Otherwise Mom and Dad will

both be mad at you at once. They might even stop letting you play outside after school."

"They should meet my daughter," Celia muttered. Jamie glanced over at her, but she was looking at her weeds.

Jamie began to dig again. She listened to the sound the three spades made together, as they each hit the ground in their own particular pattern. Digging helped her think about the conference, and she turned it over in her mind, trying to figure out where it had begun. Whatever had happened, she knew she needed to be careful for the next few days and try not to cause too many problems. She didn't feel like seeing her parents in a bad mood until she had to, which would happen soon enough.

"We should probably go soon," she told Rachel. "We don't want to be late for dinner."

"I know," Rachel said. "Let's each just do one more weed."

Jamie nodded. She wormed her fingers down into the dirt until she could feel the roots of a stiff stem. Carefully, she loosened the roots from the ground, and pulled the weed free.

Chapter Twelve

Jamie sat with Tara and Elise in their tree. Elise was drawing their invisible tree house out on a map.

"I wish the tree house was real," Elise said. "And we could build the whole thing ourselves."

Elise grinned at Jamie, but Jamie was having trouble concentrating on the tree house. She leaned back to feel the sun.

"What's wrong?" Elise asked.

"Nothing." Jamie opened her eyes. "I just don't understand why you have to go with your parents to conferences here. We never had to at my old school."

Tara glanced at Elise.

"You don't always have to," she said.

"Hmmm?" Jamie sat all the way up.

"I had to last year," Tara went on.

"Was it bad?" Jamie asked.

"Not that bad. But my mom and Mr. Atwell talked about me like I wasn't there. And then they both talked to me at the same time about what needed to change. That part wasn't too fun."

Jamie nodded.

"That's what I was worried about," she said. "And the worst thing is, I can't plan what I want to say back, because I don't know what I did."

"I guess you'll find out," Tara said.

Jamie turned to Elise.

"Do you have to go to yours with Mrs. Hazelett?" she asked.

"No," Elise said. "My parents don't usually go to conferences. They talked to my teacher on the phone last year, but that was about it."

"Wow," Jamie said. "Then they won't have to meet each other. That sounds great."

Elise looked at Jamie straight on.

"Sort of," she said. Then she let go with her hands and swung upside down by her knees. "But sometimes I wish they knew what my school looked like."

Jamie watched Elise swing. It would be one thing if Elise's parents hadn't seen her school yet this year, but Elise had been at Lookout since first grade. How could her parents have been too busy to go to that many conferences? An answer shot into Jamie's head before she could shut it out. Maybe they weren't too busy. Maybe they just didn't want to go.

Jamie sat in the backseat of the car.

"First conference at a new school, hmm Jamie?" her dad said.

"Yeah," Jamie said. And maybe the last. Maybe Mrs. Hazelett had just decided that Jamie didn't fit in at Lookout Elementary.

"Jamie?" her dad said.

"What?" Jamie said. "Sorry, I wasn't listening."

"I asked you how school was today," her dad said.

"I guess the same." She knew he wanted her to say more, but it was hard with Mrs. Hazelett on her mind.

"Well, I hope Rachel's okay alone with that sitter," he went on. "Patsy's a little strange if you ask me."

Her dad kept talking, filling the silence of the car. He always did that when they were going somewhere that made them nervous. Her mom was always quiet during those times, which made her dad talk even more.

When they finally got to the school, Jamie led her parents to Mrs. Hazelett's room. She opened the door slowly.

ELIZABETH SCARBORO

"Hi, Mrs. Hazelett," she said.

"Hi, Jamie." Mrs. Hazelett turned to Jamie's parents. "Hi, nice to have you here."

"I'm Rebecca," her mom said, shaking Mrs. Hazelett's hand.

"Jeremy," her dad said, extending his hand. "And you are . . . ?"

How could he forget a name like Mrs. Hazelett?

"Connie," she said. She smiled at Jamie. "Still Mrs. Hazelett to you."

Jamie's mom and dad sat down at the table.

"Why don't you join us, Jamie," Mrs. Hazelett said.

Jamie glanced at the table. She went to her desk and got her chair. She felt like sitting down right there, but she made herself drag the chair over to the conference table.

"Well, I've really enjoyed having Jamie in my class," Mrs. Hazelett began. "I'm sure you know what I mean. She's creative, diligent most of the time, inquisitive."

Tara was right. Not only were they talking about her like she wasn't there, they were using words she couldn't understand.

"She's a little quiet in discussion," Mrs. Hazelett went on, "but we're working on that."

"Quiet?" her dad asked. "Jamie?"

"That's new," her mom said, turning to Jamie.

"*I'm* new," Jamie said to her.

"And for someone new, you're getting used to things pretty quickly. However," Mrs. Hazelett said, turning to Jamie like her parents had left. "There are a few things we need to work on. I think you're having trouble paying attention sometimes."

Jamie nodded. How did Mrs. Hazelett know when her mind wandered?

"What's been happening?" her dad asked.

"I don't know," Jamie said. "I just start thinking about other things."

Actually, she felt like thinking about other things right now.

"I'm sure most children have trouble paying attention occasionally," her mom said.

"Yes," Mrs. Hazelett said. "And it's fine if it doesn't get in the way of their learning. But I think it's beginning to get in Jamie's way."

Here we go, Jamie thought. She raced to think of what Mrs. Hazelett was going to say before she said it, but it was no use.

"Jamie, do you realize you never turned in a special report?" Mrs. Hazelett looked right at Jamie, her eyebrows forming triangles over her eyes.

Jamie looked at the table. She wasn't sure what the special report was, but it sounded too familiar. Last week Mrs. Hazelett had called for the special reports to be turned in. Jamie had hoped they were extra-credit projects.

"Jamie?" her mom said. The tired sound was back in her voice.

"I didn't know we had to," Jamie said.

"Now, I talked about the special reports at the very beginning of the year," Mrs. Hazelett said. "They're pretty important. In fact they have their own space on your report cards. Every student does one report each quarter. I handed out a sheet listing the topics you could choose from, and the day the reports were due."

Jamie couldn't remember the sheet. But then, she put lots of sheets in her desk to look at later.

"Are you sure you gave one to everybody?" she asked.

"Yes," said Mrs. Hazelett. "And I'm sure I reminded the class when they were due a week ahead of time, and then again the day before. I don't have the time to check with each student and make sure you're all listening. Besides, I want you to learn to take care of yourselves."

Jamie had never heard a teacher sound so much like her own mom.

"Jamie," her dad said. "What do you think happened to your sheet?"

Mrs. Hazelett looked at Jamie.

"Maybe it's time to show your parents your desk," she said.

Jamie stood up slowly. How could Mrs. Hazelett do that? It wasn't fair. How would she like it if all the parents looked in her desk without asking?

"Jamie, your parents don't need to go through your things. I just want them to see what it looks like, and how it might be holding you back. You're too smart to let your messiness get in your way."

Jamie groaned to herself. Last year, her teacher had said that same thing, only it was about her handwriting.

Jamie's parents bent down to look in the large cubby space of her desk. Jamie peered in after them. With her parents there it looked far worse than normal. Her books were hidden by wrinkled papers, some of which were about to spill out onto the floor.

Her dad stood back.

"With a desk like this I'm surprised you get anything done at all," he said. His voice was low, making Jamie wish she could tell him she was sorry.

"This is worse than your clothes box," her mom said. "Your room doesn't even get this bad."

"That's because you make me clean it," Jamie said quietly. "I like it messy, but I never get the chance."

Jamie's mom looked hard at Jamie, refusing to let her look away. "What have you been doing when you're asked to clean your desk?"

Jamie tried to remember those times. Each Friday before lunch, Mrs. Hazelett gave them a chance to clean.

"On Fridays we have time," Jamie said. "But we only have to clean it if we need to. I've never really needed to."

Her mom raised one eyebrow.

"Really," she said. "So, how do you spend that time?"

"I guess I talk to Elise," Jamie said.

"But Jamie," Mrs. Hazelett said, "Elise has time to talk because she keeps her desk clean."

Jamie peered into Elise's desk. Her books were lined up next to her notebooks in the big cubby space. In the small space, her pens and pencils made two neat rows. For some reason, Elise's desk didn't seem much like Elise.

"Now there's a child whose parents taught her how to take care of her things," Jamie's mom said to her dad.

"That child teaches herself," Mrs. Hazelett said, her voice getting lower. "Now if I could talk to *those* parents—"

Mrs. Hazelett caught Jamie's eye and kept the rest of her sentence to herself.

Jamie's mom looked at Mrs. Hazelett, nodding. So Jamie had guessed right about Elise's parents, more right than she'd imagined.

"I'm sure there are lots of reasons that Jamie's gotten disorganized," Mrs. Hazelett continued. "Moving to a new city, to a new school, it can be disorienting."

Disorienting. Jamie didn't know what it meant, but it sounded like she felt.

"I'm sure that's part of it," her dad said. "But it doesn't excuse the problem."

Jamie studied her dad's shoes. She hated it when she knew he was right. She looked at her desk. She couldn't imagine how she'd ever clean the whole thing out.

"Starting this Friday, which is tomorrow, you can work on your desk," Mrs. Hazelett said. "I think it will make a difference."

"Okay," Jamie said.

"And what about her work?" Jamie's dad asked. "Why don't we help her keep track."

Mrs. Hazelett looked at Jamie.

"Why don't you try keeping all your assignments in one place?" she said. "Then you can let your parents help you check them off, or you can do it yourself if that works better."

"Okay," Jamie said.

"Which reminds me," Mrs. Hazelett said, walking back to her desk, "I have something for you."

She handed Jamie a piece of paper.

"This is the next special report assignment," she said. "This quarter you are earning an F in special reports. Hopefully you can raise your grade."

Jamie read the sheet. It listed three topic choices, but Mrs. Hazelett had already circled one for her. Jamie didn't have to look hard to figure out why. The circled choice had one phrase underlined: must read aloud to the class.

Mrs. Hazelett turned to Jamie's parents.

"I'm sorry to cut this short," she said. "But I'm already five minutes late for my next conference."

"Well, I'm glad we got the chance to talk," Jamie's dad said.

"Yes, thank you," her mom said. "Jamie's lucky to have you."

Mrs. Hazelett smiled her lipstick smile.

"The feeling's mutual," she said. "I'll see you tomorrow, Jamie."

"Bye, Mrs. Hazelett," Jamie said, following her parents out of the room.

Jamie walked behind her parents. They were talking quietly to each other and she didn't want to join the conversation. She wasn't in the mood to answer questions about her report, or her desk, or anything. Her mom slowed down until Jamie had to walk next to her. Jamie looked up.

"I've seen some messy desks, but yours tops them all," she said.

"Am I going to be grounded?" Jamie asked.

"Not as long as you get your report done," her mom said. "But I have a feeling you will."

Jamie had more than a feeling. She'd never be able to look at Mrs. Hazelett again unless she wrote that stupid report.

"Especially because we're going to try out a new plan," her dad said.

"What is it?" Jamie asked. She couldn't believe they'd come up with a plan that fast.

"For a while, you're going to do your homework before you go outside after school," he said.

"That way you won't have trouble making sure it gets done," her mom added.

She wished she could argue, but her F in special reports got in the way of all the arguments she knew.

"I have an idea," her dad said as they reached the car.

Jamie wasn't sure she was ready for another new idea.

"What is it?" she asked.

"Why don't we get Rachel and go out for ice cream?"

Jamie stared at her dad. Sometimes he had good ideas at the strangest times.

Her mom smiled.

"I like that idea," she said. "We can drop Patsy home on the way."

"As long as we don't have to talk about school," Jamie said.

Her dad shook his head.

"I think we've all had enough of school for tonight," he said.

Chapter Thirteen

Jamie lay in bed listening to the mattress wires creak softly above her. Any minute, she knew Rachel would mumble something. But for now Rachel was quiet, like she used to be when Jamie couldn't sleep. Maybe it was the ice cream. She and Jamie had both gotten double scoops. Rachel had guessed Jamie's conference must have been great when she heard about the ice cream. The whole way in the car she kept whispering, "I don't get it."

Jamie didn't get it either. She knew her parents were mad. But after they talked about the new plan they didn't ask her any more questions. They just acted like things would change.

Jamie turned over, sinking into her mattress. She just hoped she'd be able to change things. When she left Mrs. Hazelett's room, it had sounded easy. But when she pictured her desk, she couldn't imagine it empty. Tomorrow she would have to look at every single piece of paper inside it. And she would have to do it fast, because she couldn't finish after school. She and Elise needed to practice for the three-legged race.

Jamie's desk flashed away. She stirred awake to the sound of her mom's voice coming from the kitchen.

"It worries me," the voice was saying.

There was silence.

"Jamie will figure it out," her dad said. "Did you see her face when she heard about the F?"

"I know. It's not the report, even, that worries me. It's . . ."

Her mom's voice became lower, and Jamie strained to catch her words.

". . . Mrs. Hazelett described her . . . quiet. What is Jamie thinking about?"

Jamie sat up and leaned forward, trying to hear her dad's answer, but it was muffled by the sound of running water.

" . . . settled in Boulder," her mom was saying.

"But that can't be the entire . . ." her dad's words blended into the water again.

The entire what, Jamie wondered.

The water became louder, hiding the conversation from

Jamie completely. She could hear someone putting away plates in the cupboard. She lay as still as she could, waiting for them to finish the dishes.

Her dad was speaking now, his voice sounding serious. " . . . and Rachel's sleepwalking . . ."

A towel swished back and forth.

"Wish I knew why," her mom said in a worried voice.

That voice made Jamie open her eyes. When her mom talked about the sleepwalking, she had talked about it easily, like it was something lots of people did. Now Jamie wondered if she'd been acting calm about it so Rachel would stay calm. Jamie felt like jumping out of bed and telling her mom about Angie and the three-way fight, so she wouldn't have to wonder about Rachel.

Suddenly Jamie realized the kitchen was quiet. She peered under her door into the hallway. The kitchen light was still on. Just faintly, she could hear her dad's voice. He spoke too softly for her to make out his exact words, but she caught their rhythm. The words were slow and separated, like each one counted, and he was using them to figure something out. They ended in the sound of a question. Jamie heard her mom begin to answer. Her words flowed into each other, but her voice didn't sound sure enough to carry an answer in it.

Her dad spoke, and the conversation began to move

between them again. The words were indecipherable, but their feeling was clear. Both voices carried the same unsteady, sad sound underneath them. Jamie rolled over. There was nothing worse than lying in the dark and hearing her parents sound like that. It felt so terrible that it made her forget to wonder what they were sad about.

Jamie closed her eyes. She could hear her parents leaving the kitchen and coming toward her down the hall.

"I know I'll feel more settled when we've decided whether or not we're staying," her mom was saying.

Jamie heard her dad sigh.

"Maybe we should make our decision sooner than we'd planned."

"I don't see why not," her mom said. "We've been here long enough to get some sense of what it would mean to live here."

Jamie already knew her what her own sense of it was. Phoenix was okay, but it was flat. No hills, no snow, no mountains. And school was harder. She imagined going back to her old school, and telling everybody about Phoenix. She'd stand up in front of her old class during show-and-tell and tell them stories from her trip. After show-and-tell, was handwriting. She pictured sitting at her desk and pulling out her old handwriting book. She'd had it for a whole year and never really gotten to like it. At recess she'd play with Sheila and Beth, probably on the swings. Beth was a little bossy about the swings. Jamie could take a few days of the swings, and then she'd head for the bars.

Jamie jolted back awake.

"If we stay, I hope we can find a house with a nicer yard," her mom was saying.

Jamie pictured a yard full of trees like the ones in Celia's yard, or the tree at school. That tree by itself had enough branches for three of them to explore.

"Let's sleep on it," her dad was saying.

"I have tomorrow morning off," her mom said. "Maybe we can go have breakfast somewhere."

Jamie heard them walking down the hall. She wished she could sneak out of school and spy on their breakfast. Then again, she wasn't sure she wanted to hear what they had to say.

Jamie opened the front door and swung it back and forth, waiting for Rachel. For once, she was ready first. She'd thought she'd be especially tired after the conference, but for some reason she woke right up.

Rachel jumped through the door and let Jamie close it behind them.

"Jamie, did I talk in my sleep last night?"

Jamie tried to remember. Lately, Rachel talked in her sleep so often that all her murmuring blended into one long night. But now that Jamie thought about it, last night had been different.

"No," Jamie said. "I don't think you talked at all."

"I knew it!" Rachel said. "This morning, I woke up and I didn't feel tired from sleeping."

Then Jamie remembered who she had heard talking.

"I should be really tired," she said. "I stayed awake listening to Mom and Dad."

Rachel grinned.

"Did they talk about anything good?"

"I wouldn't say good," Jamie said. "They were talking about moving."

"What about moving?" Rachel asked.

"About whether we're staying or going," Jamie said.

"We're going back," Rachel said. "After a year, right?"

"I don't know," Jamie said. "Before I thought they'd pick Colorado, but now I can't tell."

She looked at Rachel.

"I thought you didn't care about going back," she said. "You wanted to move."

"I didn't want to that much. I still miss our house, and

Jessica," she said. "But then, the second-grade fight is almost over, and recess is just getting fun again. I've been playing with Sara a lot. Maybe if we went back I'd have to start missing her."

Jamie remembered her own recesses.

"I know," she said.

Rachel tilted her head and glanced at Jamie sideways.

"And there's Celia," she said.

They turned the corner at the cul-de-sac, heading for the bus stop. Jamie dug her hands deep in her pockets, smoothing out their linings. She watched the pebbles jump out from the wheels of a passing truck.

"I know," she said.

Chapter Fourteen

"Okay," Mrs. Hazelett said. "We have half an hour until lunchtime. If you need to clean your desks you should work on that now. If your desk is clean you may talk quietly to your neighbor."

Elise turned to Jamie.

"How was your conference?" she asked.

"Not great," Jamie said. "For one thing, my parents saw my desk."

"So?" Elise asked. She leaned over and peered into Jamie's cubbies.

"Wow," she said.

"I guess I have to clean it out today," Jamie said.

"I guess so," Elise said, still staring into Jamie's desk.

"What else happened?"

Jamie pulled out a handful of crumpled papers. She looked at them, trying to remember what they were.

"And I never turned in a special report," she said.

"How come?" Elise asked. She was asking more questions than usual.

"I didn't know we had to," Jamie said.

"So what are you going to do?" Elise asked.

Jamie pulled out a few more papers. This handful, she could tell, was from the beginning of school.

"Well, Mrs. Hazelett gave me the list for this quarter's report," she said. She glanced at Elise. "I have to read mine to the class."

Elise looked at Jamie. Jamie remembered when Elise read her last book report to the class. She'd changed the words of the report a little, enough to make the class laugh and still not get in trouble.

"Hmm," Elise said. "That sounds like Mrs. Hazelett."

Jamie nodded, still staring at the papers now covering her desk.

"I'd better hurry," she said. "Otherwise Mrs. Hazelett will make me stay after school, and we need all the time we can get to practice for our race."

She unfolded a few of the papers to get a better look at

them. Most of them were already graded. Two, unfortunately, were math assignments from this week. She tried to smooth out their wrinkles.

"Hey, Jamie?" Elise said.

"Yeah?" Jamie looked up from her pile.

"Well—" Elise stopped. Mrs. Hazelett was standing over Jamie's desk.

"How is it coming?" she asked Jamie.

"Fine," Jamie said, stretching her arm out over her new math assignments.

"Good," she said. She looked at Elise. "I don't want any distractions. Unless you're talking about cleaning, you can save your conversations for recess."

She turned around, and Elise rolled her eyes at Jamie. Jamie smiled and shot a ball of paper into the basket. One down, at least fifty to go.

Elise pulled a book out of her desk.

"Tell me when you're done," she said.

"We'll be in fifth grade before that," Jamie said.

"On second thought," Elise said, "just tell me when it's time for lunch."

Jamie waited for Elise to finish her lunch. She was eating her sandwich too slowly, stopping between bites.

"Come on," Jamie told her. "Tara's probably wondering where we are."

Elise nodded.

"You're right," she said. She folded her napkin into a fan, and put it carefully in her lunchbox.

Jamie stood and walked to the door, with Elise following behind her.

Tara was waiting for them outside the door.

"My class got out early today," she said. "Come on, let's go climb the tree."

Elise walked slowly, until Tara looked at her. Elise shook her head. Then she looked at Jamie. Jamie looked back at Elise, and then at Tara. Their faces had a similar expression, and something about it made Jamie feel like leaving to play four-square.

"Jamie," Elise said. "Tara talked to Mr. Bixbie, and . . . well, he said when you get to fourth grade you can choose partners from any class for the three-legged race."

Jamie glanced at Tara. She was looking at Jamie closely. Jamie stared at the tree behind her, picking out her favorite branch.

"See," Tara said. "It's just that we've been wanting to be partners for two years and we've never been in the same class."

Jamie nodded, watching Tara's left shoe dig its way into the dirt. She looked up at Tara's scabbed knees. Elise probably knew exactly when Tara had fallen to get each of those cuts, the way Jamie knew all about the two warts on Sheila's knees. Sheila had tried at least twenty times to make them disappear, and Jamie had been there for most of those attempts. Jamie tried to imagine a new girl coming to be friends with her and Sheila. They'd ask her to swing with them and join their spy club. But there would be too many things she'd never know. And Jamie and Sheila would have fun at recess, whether the girl was with them or not.

"I know you asked me first," Elise was saying. "And it's only fair if you still want to. But we were wondering if you'd mind changing."

Mind changing to what? Jamie wondered. But she looked right at Elise.

"Yeah," Jamie said. "You guys go ahead."

"We can be partners for other things," Elise said.

Jamie shrugged. Maybe, maybe not, as far as she was concerned.

"Thanks," Tara said.

Jamie looked up at her. She wasn't smiling, at least. Jamie glanced at the four-square game. Somehow, that didn't even look fun right now.

"Want to go up in the tree?" Tara asked.

Elise looked at Jamie.

"I'm going to go play tetherball," Jamie said. "See you when the bell rings."

She left before they could answer, walking as fast as she could without looking like she needed to run. She walked past the four-square, past the tunnel, to where the tetherballs hung silent.

She picked up the yellow ball and swung it hard, then turned and hit it in the opposite direction. At first she hit lightly, giving herself time to turn and hit it the other way, keeping the game going. But who really cared about the game? She hit harder, until she was only hitting in one direction, making the ball fly in smaller circles, winding its rope tighter and tighter around the pole.

Chapter Fifteen

"I'll be your partner," Rachel said as they walked away from the bus.

"You can't," Jamie said. "You're not in my grade."

Rachel walked close to Jamie.

"Besides," Jamie told her, "I don't want to be in it anymore."

"Did you get mad at them?" Rachel asked.

Jamie pictured Elise telling her it was only fair for them to be partners. If she'd gotten mad, Elise would have known it mattered and probably raced with Jamie, just to be fair. And Jamie would have to spend the race knowing Elise would rather be with Tara.

"Not really," she told Rachel.

She walked slowly, kicking two different rocks along with

her. She tried to pass one to Rachel, but it rolled up onto the grass. She kept the other going, all the way to their sidewalk. She let the rock roll into the street, and followed Rachel through their front door into the kitchen.

"Hi girls," their dad said, coming in from the back porch.

"Hi Dad," Rachel said. "I thought today was the day Mom got home early."

"Well, my afternoon was freed up," he said. "So I decided to come home early myself. Besides, I wanted to be here to see the beginning of the new plan in action."

Jamie stared at him. She'd forgotten all about her promise to do her homework right away. She imagined sitting in her room, trying to do her math. Each time she'd look at a problem, she'd picture the tetherball instead.

"I don't have very much homework," Jamie began.

Her dad got out the tuna fish and started to fix himself a sandwich.

"Then you'll have plenty of time to go outside after you finish," he said.

"Dad, it's not the right time to do my homework," Jamie said. "I can tell already, I won't be able to do it."

He sat down at the kitchen table.

"There's never a right time," he said.

"Dad," Jamie tried one last time.

"Jamie, I'm serious about this," he said. "Have a snack, and then it's time for your homework."

Jamie took some cheese crackers out of the cupboard.

"As long as I'm here," he said, "why don't I make you a real snack?"

Jamie sat down at the table. She wasn't planning on sitting down at all, but with one of her parents in the kitchen, she couldn't get away with taking her food into her room.

"No thanks," Jamie told him. "This is what I want."

"I'll take a snack," Rachel said.

"How about tuna?" her dad asked.

"Great," Rachel said. She sat down next to Jamie.

Jamie searched through the newspaper for the comics. Out of the corner of her eye, she caught her mom walking toward the table.

"Hi, girls," she said.

"Hi, Mom," Jamie mumbled, trying to read the guide to the newspaper on the front page.

"Jamie, your dad's making tuna fish," her mom began.

Jamie looked up at her.

"I know!" she said. "Why does everyone want me to eat tuna fish?"

"Because it's real food, unlike cheese crackers, and someone is making it right here in the kitchen," her mom answered.

Jamie glared across Rachel at her mom. She couldn't stand it when her mom answered a question she wasn't really asking. Her dad came over to the table, carrying two bowls of tuna fish. He set one down in front of Rachel and sat down across from them.

"Dad!" Jamie said.

"Don't worry," he said. "It's not for you, it's for me."

Jamie opened the comics and looked for her favorites.

"Jamie," her dad said. "Is something wrong?"

Jamie looked up at her dad. She met his eyes but she couldn't find her voice to say no. She shrugged.

Rachel glanced at Jamie, and then took a bite of her tuna fish.

"Did something happen at school?" he asked, settling into his side of the booth.

Jamie studied the back of the box of crackers. Something had happened, all right. Something she hadn't expected. But how could she know what to expect in Phoenix? At her old school, if Sheila was going to trade partners, she'd have felt it coming. And Sheila wouldn't have traded, because they were the perfect partners. They were even the same height.

"I wish I could do the three-legged race at my old school," Jamie said.

Her dad nodded.

"Sheila and I were going to do it together again this year," she said. "Last year, we beat everybody."

"I remember you practicing in the backyard," her dad said.

Jamie flipped a cheese cracker back and forth, watching her fingertips turn bright orange.

"Maybe they have the three-legged race here," her mom said, coming to sit down.

"I don't want to do it here," she said.

If she raced here, she'd get stuck with someone she didn't know at all. She'd just have to wait till next year, and then maybe she and Sheila would get a second chance. But she didn't even know about that.

She looked up at her dad, who was looking at her mom.

"When are you going to know?" she asked.

Her dad looked at her. He put his fork down, and leaned over his plate, resting his elbows on the table.

"If we're moving," Jamie said, louder. "When are you going to know?"

"We've been thinking a lot about it," her mom said. "We'd planned to take you out tomorrow night to talk about it. But maybe we should talk about it now."

Jamie stared at her. When they'd left Colorado, her dad

had said they could talk about it. And they'd talked about it, and even though she'd said she didn't want to go, they'd gone.

Jamie closed the box of crackers. She stood up on the bench and stepped over Rachel.

"I don't want to talk about Phoenix," she said.

She walked down the hall. Her dad would just have to be mad when he figured out she'd gone outside. She opened the front door quietly so that even Rachel wouldn't follow her out. Then she ran to the end of the block and turned the corner. If she were in Colorado right now she'd knock on Sheila's window, and Sheila would come out without asking any questions. They'd walk all the way across town and stay out long enough to make their parents worry.

Jamie looked across the street. She could barely walk ten blocks without getting lost, much less make her way across town. Still, maybe today was the day to try. She turned the corner. She would just keep walking until she felt like she was far enough away. Then she remembered one place that felt far away from everything. Celia had said she was welcome any time.

Jamie walked toward Celia's dark blue house. She thought about the first time she'd met Celia. "You must miss your home," Celia had said, and Jamie never got to answer but she could tell that Celia understood.

She headed into the oleander passageway. Maybe this time she'd tell Celia everything: about still being new, about the three-legged race, about Elise and Tara. She'd tell her about being so mad she couldn't even get mad, about sitting next to Elise and trying to act like it was no big deal. Celia would ask her questions, maybe even help her figure out what she should do, if it was still worth it to try and be Elise's friend. Celia had moved before, and maybe she'd met people like Elise and Tara, who were already best friends before she got there.

Jamie came to the opening in the oleanders, and stepped into the garden. Celia was sitting at the far edge of the garden, her back to the passageway. Jamie couldn't see her hands, but she was sure Celia was weeding.

"Hi," Jamie called out to her. "I hope it's okay that I'm here."

Celia spun around and Jamie jumped back. She wasn't Celia at all. She was the tall woman who had been in the garden when Jamie and Rachel had been spying. The woman stood up quickly, and walked over to Jamie. She was carrying the red-handled spade. Jamie looked at the woman's hands. They were covered with dirt. Jamie was sure she'd heard the woman say she didn't care about the garden. In fact, she'd tried to keep Celia away from the garden altogether.

"My name is Jamie," Jamie said quickly. She held her arms close to her stomach and glanced back at the oleander path. Celia had joked that this woman would chase them home if she saw them, and Jamie wondered if she was partly serious.

"I thought you were Celia," she went on, talking more and more quickly, "and I come to see her sometimes, I mean, she told me I could—"

"Don't worry," the woman interrupted. "My mother's told me all about you. I'm Celia's daughter Laura."

Jamie stared up at the woman. The woman's eyes were blue, but much lighter blue than Celia's. Her eyebrows jumped out like thick dark lines, and her eyes looked small underneath them. Her jaw stuck out a tiny bit, making her look like her teeth were clenched together. Nothing about her face reminded Jamie of Celia. Then again, Jamie had never seen Celia frown the way Laura was frowning.

"You're Celia's daughter?" Jamie asked.

"Yes," Laura said. She turned the spade handle slowly back and forth, like she was thinking about what to do with it.

"Do you like to work in her garden, too?" Jamie tried to sound like she thought it could be true.

Laura smiled. Her mouth curved slowly, and for some reason it made Jamie sad.

"No," she said. "And I'm terrible at it. But Mother won't rest until it gets done, so I want to help her finish it."

Jamie looked up at Laura. She wondered if Laura knew that Celia liked to weed the garden herself, even if it took her a long time to get it done.

"Is she here?" Jamie asked.

"Yes," said Laura. "She's coming out in a minute. She doesn't feel well enough to garden herself today, but I'm sure she'll be happy to see you."

"What's wrong?" Jamie asked.

Laura caught Jamie's eyes. This time Jamie looked back at her slowly, and she noticed that Laura's eyes were getting bigger. Jamie looked down to let Laura blink back her tear in private.

"We're not sure," Laura murmured, looking past Jamie. "These past few days she's had trouble eating, and she can barely stay awake. She thinks she just has the flu, but I don't know. The doctor warned her last month to get more rest . . ."

Laura glanced at Jamie suddenly, like she'd forgotten she was talking out loud.

"I keep trying to tell her," Laura said. "But she doesn't believe me."

Jamie nodded, but she felt a little guilty, thinking back to the first time she saw Laura. She hadn't believed Laura either, when she and Rachel saw her trying to tell Celia to rest. She'd been sure Laura was getting in the way of Celia's gardening, and wished she'd mind her own business.

"I hope she'll be okay," Jamie said. She looked at the flowers by her feet. Celia was probably right that she had the flu. But why would the doctor warn her?

The door beneath the ivy creaked open.

"Hello, Jamie."

Jamie looked up as Celia walked toward them. She felt a flash of heat as she remembered why she'd come to the garden in the first place. She remembered her parents in the kitchen, and Elise and Tara on the playground. She thought about the way the tetherball looked swinging around the pole faster and faster as she hit it again and again.

"I'll go bring out some lemonade," Laura said, heading quickly inside the house.

Celia sat down in the white chair, and Jamie sat down in the grass next to her.

"Jamie, what's wrong?" Celia said, leaning down close to her.

Jamie looked at the red and yellow flowers, thinking about where she should start. Then she looked up at Celia. Celia's face was paler than normal, and Jamie could see the bones beneath her cheeks too easily. But her cheeks were nothing compared to her eyes. Celia's eyes were more gray than blue. Instead of pulling Jamie in close to them, they sat with the stillness of a lake, leaving Jamie on her own.

Celia reached for Jamie's hand.

"You look like you had a rough day in school," she said.

Jamie thought about her fight with Elise and Tara. She looked down at Celia's hand. She felt a trembling, buried under the bones of Celia's fingers. Celia probably wanted to pick up the spade by her feet more than anything, but she would have to wait. And she didn't know how long she would have to wait. Holding Celia's hand, Jamie's nervous feeling about Elise seemed small. Even her fight with her parents, even not knowing whether she'd move or not, seemed smaller than Celia's hand.

"Yeah," Jamie said. "It was a pretty bad day. For some reason I was fighting with everybody."

Celia kept her fingers curled around Jamie's.

"How about you?" Jamie said.

"I suppose I was fighting today, too," she said. "But I'm fighting off the flu, and luckily the flu can't talk back to you, so you can say anything you want to it."

Jamie smiled. But she couldn't help noticing the way

Celia sat, like something heavy was pushing down on her chest.

"Is your daughter staying here?" Jamie asked.

"Yes." Celia sighed. "She's insisting on it."

For once Jamie was glad that Celia's daughter was pushy enough to get her way. She squeezed Celia's hand as they sat together in silence, waiting for their lemonade.

Jamie could see Rachel sitting on the sidewalk in front of their house. When she spotted Jamie coming, she walked to meet her in the middle of the cul-de-sac.

"Celia's sick," Jamie said.

"Really sick?" Rachel looked up at Jamie.

"I don't know," Jamie said. "She came out to sit in the garden, but when I left she was about to go lie down in bed."

"I wish we could help her get better," Rachel said.

"Me, too," Jamie said.

She walked next to Rachel, balancing on the curb. She slowed down as they came to the corner.

"The worst part is picturing her inside," she said. "She's used to sitting under her tree, watching her flowers."

Rachel stopped. She looked at Jamie.

"That's something we can do," she said.

"What?" Jamie asked her.

"We can bring her plants."

Jamie smiled. It was the first good idea she'd heard all day.

"That's it," she told Rachel. "That's what she'd want."

"I wish we could bring her one now," Rachel said. "I feel like seeing her."

"She's resting," Jamie told her. "But her daughter said we could come the day after tomorrow." Jamie couldn't help sighing. That would be Sunday, the day before she had to go back to school and see Elise.

"It's almost dinnertime, anyway," Rachel said.

Jamie slowed down, watching her shoes miss the cracks in the sidewalk.

"Are they mad?" she asked.

"They were mad when you left," Rachel said. "Then they seemed sort of sad."

Jamie remembered the sound of their voices as she was lying in the dark.

"Did they come look for me?"

"No." Rachel slowed down to match Jamie's steps. "I said you probably went to visit Celia."

Jamie looked at Rachel. They'd told their parents about Celia once, but that was in the very beginning.

"What did they say?" Jamie asked.

"Mom said she was glad Celia's around."

Jamie stopped. Her parents didn't even know about Celia, about her garden, her trips to different countries, her daughter, her sickness. But for the first time, Jamie considered telling them.

"What's for dinner?" she asked Rachel.

"I don't know," Rachel said. "But it's not one thing."

"What's that?"

"Cheese crackers," Rachel said. "Dad threw the whole box in the trash."

Jamie laughed. Rachel smiled, walking faster. Jamie sped up to keep Rachel's pace as the two of them headed home.

Chapter Sixteen

Jamie walked out the back of the Biltmore Hotel toward a huge flower garden. She hadn't expected to see a garden in a place like this. It was strange to see people sitting at fancy tables right in the garden paths, like the flowers were just there for them to look at while they ate dinner. The flowers looked lonely, spread apart into neat rows, unable to spill into each other.

Jamie followed her parents to the gigantic fountain in the middle of the garden. The fountain was made of circles of water on top of each other, flowing into one big pool at the bottom. It looked like a clear, rushing cake, lit up by candletips of light.

Jamie looked up at her parents. The buzzing in her stomach grew stronger. This wasn't the kind of place they usually went on Saturday night. It was too fancy, and quiet.

They sat at a table next to the fountain.

"Well, girls," her mom said, "I know you've been wondering a lot about our plans for next year."

Jamie looked at Rachel. Rachel just shrugged, but Jamie could see that her eyes were dark.

"We decided to go ahead and make a decision, so that no one has to spend the next month worrying."

"What is it?" Rachel asked.

But Jamie already knew. She had known since her stomach had started buzzing, since she'd seen the garden and the fountain and the mansion-like hotel.

"We talked about it a lot," her dad said. "And we've decided we're going to stay."

Jamie pressed her fingers into the edges of the black iron table. She listened to the fountain, waiting for someone to know what to say.

"How come?" Rachel asked.

"You know I've been trying out a new job, working with Mr. Harrison," her dad said. "So far it's going pretty well. I'm just beginning to get a feel for it, and I'd like to see how it will go. In the long run, it will help us out as a family. So that's one reason."

Jamie looked at her fingers, studying the lines imprinted on them from the table. She didn't know what her dad was doing at his job, but she knew what he meant about just get-ting the feel for something. That was Phoenix all over the place.

"And this will be a better place for me to go back to school," her mom said.

Jamie remembered hearing her mom talking about want-ing to go back to school in Colorado. But it never actually happened.

"Will we ever go back?" Rachel asked.

"We'll go back to visit," her dad said, "hopefully as early as this summer."

Jamie looked at him. If you want to go all that way to visit, she thought, you must like it enough to want to live there. But there was no point in trying to explain that now.

Jamie pictured driving all the way to Colorado, from the desert to the mountains, from Fourteenth Street in Phoenix straight back to their old house. She pictured shortening Fourteenth Street with her bare hands. She'd squeeze out the space in between until she could walk from her new school to her old house, as easily as she walked from her new home to Celia's.

"They are two beautiful places," her mom said. "I wish we could have them both."

Jamie looked at her mom. Of course she thought Phoenix

was beautiful. It was easy for her. She could stay in Phoenix without having to worry about getting an F in special reports. She didn't have to wonder whether Celia was going to be okay. She didn't even know Celia. She didn't have to miss the three-legged race, and know there was someone far away who wanted to be her partner. And her mom didn't have to go back to school on Monday to face two friends who didn't need her around.

"What's so beautiful about Phoenix?" Jamie said.

She felt her face getting hot. She pulled her knees to her chest and put her head on top of them. Her dad stretched his arm around her shoulder. She let her knees drop to lean against him, and pressed her face into his white shirt, getting it wet.

Jamie felt Rachel's fingers drum against her leg. Rachel leaned against her mom, quiet, studying the flowers. Jamie closed her eyes, letting herself sink into her dad, waiting for her throat to be ready to talk again.

Chapter Seventeen

Rachel knocked on Celia's front door.

"Hello," Laura said, opening the door for them. Jamie walked through as evenly as she could, carrying the plant they'd bought with their mom. The hallway was dark, and it took her a minute to be able to see the walls clearly. She tried to look straight ahead, imagining that she was carrying a huge, light pillow.

Rachel tapped on Celia's door, and pushed it open a crack. She peeked her head in, and then turned to Jamie.

"Celia's resting," she said.

"Let's just go in," Jamie said. She could feel the blood moving out of her hands, like it used to when she made snowballs without her mittens on.

"She said to come to her room."

Rachel pushed the door open and stepped inside. Jamie

followed her, and put the plant on Celia's bedside table while she took in Celia's room. Celia had pictures of her family on her dresser and paintings of red flowers on the wall facing her bed. The room felt crowded and empty at the same time.

Jamie glanced at Rachel, but Rachel was standing in the corner, waiting for Jamie to make the first move. Jamie walked up to Celia's bed. She watched Celia's sheet drift up and down over her chest. The room was still except for the sheet, and Jamie wasn't sure she wanted to interrupt the quiet. She looked at Celia's face.

Celia's mouth was open a little, and her skin looked soft over the bones of her cheeks. Her eyebrows bunched low over her eyes. Jamie had never seen Celia frown before. She pictured her dreaming about a fight, working hard even while she slept.

"Come on, aren't you going to wake her up?" Rachel whispered.

Jamie nodded.

"I am, I am," she said.

She touched Celia on the shoulder.

Celia opened her eyes.

"Jamie," she said.

She lifted her head up to peer past Jamie's waist.

"And Rachel," she said.

Rachel came to stand by her bed.

"Hi Celia," Rachel said. She put her hand on Celia's hair and forehead, like she used to do to their grandma.

"That feels good," Celia said. "How did you manage to keep your hand so nice and cool, out there in the sun?"

"We haven't been in the sun," Rachel said. "We went somewhere special."

Jamie groaned. Rachel couldn't hold a secret in for more than five minutes—three minutes if it was a good one.

"Where was that?" Celia asked.

"Here," Jamie said, "you have to be sitting up before we can tell you."

Celia lifted her head, letting Jamie prop her pillows up against her headboard. Then she pushed herself up to lean against them. Jamie was glad to see Celia sitting, even if she was in bed.

"We went to the nursery," she said, picking up the dark green plant with yellow flowers to show her.

Celia's eyes opened all the way. As Celia looked at the flowers, Jamie thought she saw the blue growing in the middle of her eyes, pushing the gray to the outside rims.

"That's beautiful," she said. "I haven't seen one of these in years."

"The flowers are the same colors as yours outside," Rachel said.

Celia smiled.

"It makes me feel like I'm outside just to see them."

Jamie's head felt light. She hadn't noticed how heavy it'd been all morning until now.

"How did you girls get that all the way here?" Celia asked.

"Our mom drove us," Jamie said. "She took us to the nursery."

"You can hang it from your ceiling," Rachel said. "That way, when you lie in bed, you can watch it."

"I'll have my daughter hang it as soon as she can," Celia said.

"We'll come and water it," Jamie said.

"That'd be nice," Celia said. "But don't worry if you forget. My daughter and I can always fill in."

Jamie nodded.

Celia looked at the girls, letting her eyes rest on each one alone. Jamie felt the room slow down, like the minutes wouldn't pass by until Celia herself told them to go ahead.

"Thank you," Celia said. "It's nice to have something alive in the room with me. Maybe now I can be more patient about getting well."

Jamie glanced at Celia's crocheted bedspread. It was made of white roses, and some of the roses were torn in the middle. She'd been planning on being patient herself, but she had to say it before Rachel did.

"Guess what else?" she said. "We're staying here."

Celia squeezed Jamie's hand.

"Really," she said. "That's lucky. I wasn't looking forward to saying good-bye to you two."

"Me neither," Jamie said.

"Now we can help you plant the summer plants when it's time," Rachel said.

Celia smiled.

"That will be nice," she said.

Rachel nudged Jamie's shoulder. Jamie looked up. Celia's eyes were beginning to close, and her head sank back into the pillows Jamie had arranged.

"Celia," she said. "Maybe we better go."

Celia opened her eyes.

"I'm sorry, girls," she said.

"Don't worry," Rachel said. "We'll be back soon."

She squeezed Celia's hand.

Jamie watched Celia shift under her covers. Her body seemed so small that it made Jamie want to hug her to make sure she was there. But she was afraid to hug her too.

Rachel went up to the bed and looked at Celia's hair for a long time. Then she stood on her toes and bent down over Celia, hugging her whole top half at once.

"Good-bye, Rachel," Celia said.

Then she lifted her arm up to Jamie.

Jamie bent down and hugged her hard, telling her arms not to hold on too long. Without thinking she kissed Celia's forehead.

"Bye, Celia," she said. "See you soon."

Then she slipped out of the room, as Celia's "Good-bye, Jamie" faded into the darkness of the hallway.

Chapter Eighteen

Jamie got off the bus slowly. All she could think about was sitting next to Elise. It'd been hard enough to sit next to her after recess on Friday, but now it was Monday, and she had a whole week ahead. She couldn't ignore Elise for that long.

Jamie dug her hand into her pocket, running her fingers over the letter she'd started to Sheila yesterday. She was hoping to finish it today during recess, in the library. She pulled it out.

Dear Sheila, Things are different here. Rachel didn't walk in her sleep at all last week. Our friend Celia is sick, but we don't know how sick. ~~Is~~ Did you have Track and Field yet? We are having ours but ~~and field~~ the races are boring here.

She had meant to tell Sheila about the three-legged race, but she couldn't figure out how to say it. It would have been easier if she knew she was leaving Phoenix. Then she wouldn't be lying when she said it didn't matter. But the race did matter. She'd done it so often before that practicing felt like home. She'd thought Elise knew that. But if she knew, she sure did a good job of ignoring it.

Jamie walked into class and sat down.

"Hi, Jamie," Elise said.

"Hi," Jamie said, reaching in her desk for her pencil.

"Listen, are you still mad about the race?"

Jamie shrugged.

"I just wanted to do it is all," she said.

"Maybe we could do another race," Elise said. "See, the three-legged race is my and Tara's favorite."

"Maybe," Jamie said. "But I don't really like any others."

Elise looked at Jamie.

"Why does it have to be such a big deal?" she said.

Jamie stared at her. She was the one who was making it bigger than it was.

"Never mind," Jamie said. "I don't want to do it here anyway. It was my favorite at my old school, but it was probably more fun there."

"Yeah," Elise muttered. "Like everything else."

Jamie glanced over at her. She tried to remember what she'd told Elise about Colorado. She wished, right now, she could tell her she was going back.

"Girls, if you don't mind, the rest of us would like to begin." Mrs. Hazelett's eyes drilled into Jamie's.

Jamie and Elise sat up.

"We're going to begin today with math," Mrs. Hazelett continued. "So please get out your homework."

Jamie reached into her backpack and pulled out her new organizer folder—her mom's idea. She found her math paper, still unwrinkled after two days.

"Stephanie, why don't you read the first problem."

Stephanie read in her perfectly clear voice. Of course, she'd gotten the problem right. Jamie felt like rolling her eyes at Elise, but she kept her eyes on her own paper. She thought she felt Elise turn toward her.

Jamie looked carefully at her answers as different people read the problems aloud. By the time they were at the end of the page, she'd only missed three. Not bad, considering they were word problems. She passed her paper to the front.

"Now, class, before we go on to reading, I want to say something about parent conferences," said Mrs. Hazelett. "I'm really happy to have had the chance to meet all of your parents. And I hope your parents have a better idea of what

we do here in our classroom. Now that they've had an intro-
duction, it's your job to keep them informed. Unless you tell
them what you're doing, they don't know how to help you
out."

Jamie sat back with relief. She had a whole quarter before
her parents would meet with Mrs. Hazelett again.

Stephanie whirled around in her chair.

"Elise," she hissed. "My mom says your mom missed her
conference again." She shook her head like a disappointed
parent. "How will she know how to help you out?"

Jamie glanced over at Elise, waiting for her comeback. But
Elise's eyes were frozen on her paper.

Jamie looked at Stephanie evenly.

"You need help more than anybody," Jamie said. "Help
learning to mind your own business."

"Look who's talking about help," Stephanie said. "Your
desk is the messiest I've ever seen."

Jamie felt like reaching forward and punching Stephanie
in the mouth so she'd shut up.

"Who cares? And who asked you to look in my desk?"
Jamie said. Then she sat back in her chair. "But I guess you're
even nosier than your nosy mother."

Stephanie opened her mouth but nothing came out.

Mrs. Hazelett walked over to Stephanie's desk.

"Stephanie, I don't remember giving you permission to turn around and talk to your neighbor," she said softly. "I'm beginning to think you've already forgotten our conference."

She raised her eyebrows, and then turned slowly and walked back to the front of the room.

Elise nudged Jamie's leg. Jamie looked over at her. She slid her spelling paper toward Jamie's desk. Jamie leaned close to Elise so that she could read the bottom of the page. In small neat letters, were the words

thank you

Jamie looked up. Elise caught her eye and she shrugged. She pulled Elise's paper on her desk and answered the note.

Elise squinted and then smiled as she read

no big deal

Jamie walked with Elise toward their tree. Tara met them as they reached the grass.

"Hi," she said. She looked at Jamie. "I didn't know if you were going to make it."

Jamie remembered her plans for recess. How did Tara know she'd considered staying in the library?

"Yeah," Jamie said. "I changed my mind."

"Good," said Tara. "We're not used to only having two people up here. On Friday it was hard to think of something to do."

"Well it looks like I'll be here a lot," Jamie said. "My parents decided we're staying in Phoenix."

Tara grinned.

"That's great," she said.

"I didn't know that," Elise said. "How come you didn't tell me this morning?"

Jamie raised her eyebrows.

"Oh yeah," Elise said. "I forgot about this morning."

"What happened?" Tara asked.

Elise looked at Jamie.

"We were fighting," Jamie said. "But Stephanie interrupted us."

"Stephanie?" Tara asked.

"Yeah. She said something so stupid we had to stop."

"What did she say?" Tara asked.

"She said something about my mom not coming to conferences," Elise said.

Tara sighed.

"She has the biggest mouth. Next to her mom, that is."

Elise smiled.

"That's what Jamie told her."

Tara laughed.

"I'm glad someone told her," she said. "She's been asking for that for a long time."

Elise held her hands out, and Tara stepped up. Jamie followed her and climbed out onto her branch.

"So you're really staying?" Elise said.

Jamie nodded.

"Do you miss Colorado?" Elise asked.

Jamie looked at her.

"Sometimes," she said. "Sometimes I wish I could put both places together and have one city."

"BoulderPhoenix," said Tara.

"Or Bouldix," Elise said. "Or Phoender."

Jamie laughed.

"Phoender? Sounds like an evil villain."

"You're right," Elise said, swinging upside down.

Jamie watched Elise's hair move below her, wrinkling slowly with the wind. She hooked her own feet under and bent backwards till her hair fell off her shoulders. She rocked, watching the upside-down playground tilt back and forth, back and forth below.

Chapter Nineteen

Jamie stood on the sidewalk watching Rachel tie her shoe.

"Hurry up," she said. "Mom thinks we're coming right home from school today, so we should try to get to Celia's fast."

Rachel scowled up at her.

"Why do we have to come right home?"

"My special report is due tomorrow. I thought Mom forgot all about it, but this morning she asked to see it. When she found out I hadn't started yet she gave me the 'grounded' look."

Rachel stood up.

"Maybe we should wait and see Celia another day."

Jamie pictured Celia in her bed.

"Don't you want to see how she's doing?"

"I do," Rachel said. "It's just, it's kind of scary, seeing her when she's lying in bed."

Jamie looked at Rachel. It'd been hard to stand over Celia's bed for very long without wanting to leave her room. But then, the minute they left the house, Jamie had wanted to go back. Either way, it didn't feel right.

They reached Celia's yard.

"I guess we should just knock on the front door again," Jamie said.

Rachel folded her arms across her chest, watching the oleander path.

Jamie walked to the front door, and knocked lightly. She hoped Laura would talk to them for a minute when she answered the door, so they wouldn't have to listen to their footsteps as they walked down the hall to Celia's room. She leaned close to the windows, but she couldn't see any movement behind the shades.

"Where is she?" Rachel said.

Jamie knocked again.

"Maybe Celia's asleep, and Laura's sitting with her."

She knew Celia had told them to come in, but she wanted to wait in case Laura came to the door first.

"I guess we should go in," Rachel said. She came to stand next to Jamie.

Jamie took a deep breath and turned the doorknob. She pushed gently, trying to be a quiet as possible. Then she pushed harder. She turned as far right as she could and pushed again. Still, the door wouldn't budge.

"What's wrong?" Rachel asked.

"It's locked," Jamie said.

"But Celia doesn't lock her door, unless she's gone," Rachel said. "Where could she go?"

Jamie remembered helping Celia sit up in bed. It took all of Celia's energy just to change positions. She wouldn't leave the house unless she really had to go somewhere. Jamie looked at Celia's window shade. She didn't want to tell Rachel where she thought Celia had gone. She looked over at Rachel, but Rachel was busy moving toward the oleanders.

"Come on," Jamie said. "We can come back later."

"I want to check the garden," Rachel said. "Just to make sure."

Jamie thought about saying no, but she knew Rachel wouldn't give up. She followed Rachel through the oleander passageway, stepping on twigs to hear them break. As they neared the edge of the clearing, Rachel slowed down.

"Celia?" she said into the garden. She took a deep breath.

Jamie stepped out of the oleanders. Celia was sitting in

her white iron chair. She rested her head in her arms on the table top as Laura weeded the flowers by her feet.

"Girls!" Celia said, lifting her head to look up at them. "I'm so glad you came over. Rachel, did you run all the way here?"

Rachel stood close to Celia.

"We thought you'd be in bed, but your front door was locked. We didn't know where you were," she said in a low voice.

"Oh dear," Celia said. "Of course you wouldn't know that I lock the door when I garden. You've always come around through the bushes."

She studied Rachel's face, and then took her hand. Jamie watched Laura, waiting. Soon she sat up from her weeding, and turned around to face the rest of them. Laura's eyes were back to their normal size, but right underneath them, her face looked swollen.

"I should have thought of that," Laura said. "I had a feeling you'd come by today."

"You did?" Celia said.

Laura rolled her eyes.

"The last time they saw you, you couldn't get out of bed."

Celia nodded.

"You looked pretty sick," Rachel said. "You look better today." She looked closely at Celia. "Well, not all the way better, but a little better."

"Who are you, the doctor?" Jamie muttered. She studied Celia's face herself. Celia's eyes were bluer again, but her face still looked too thin. Jamie wondered, between the blueness of Celia's eyes, and the thinness of her cheeks, which was there to stay.

Celia smiled. "That sounds about right," she said. "I was finally able to get out of bed this morning, but I still feel like I might have to climb back in. And I'm not well enough to do the weeding, that's for sure."

She looked at Laura.

"I tell you, though, I know it sounds like a cliché, but it feels good to be alive."

Jamie looked at Celia. Something about the word "alive" made her stomach turn. Then she remembered Mrs. Hazelett's words: "Imagine that your pencil is alive." That was it—her special report assignment. She jumped up.

"What's wrong?" Rachel asked.

"My special report," she said. "Shoot. I wish I could stay longer." She looked around the garden. It felt good to say that and actually mean it.

"Jamie's in trouble, since her report's due tomorrow," Rachel told Celia. "My mom told her to come right home from school."

Celia smiled.

"Well, being a mother myself, I can understand that," she said.

"And being a daughter," Laura said, "I'd say you better get going."

Jamie glanced over at her. Laura's smile spread across her entire face, and Jamie could see a way that her eyes might look like Celia's. She wondered if she'd ever get to see Laura make another joke. She tried to memorize her face, just in case that was the only one.

"We'll come back and help you weed," Jamie said.

"Good-bye," Celia said, watching them as they made their way to the oleanders. Jamie stopped at the edge of the oleander path, and looked back. Celia had begun to motion to Laura, who shook her head as she weeded the flowers. At the rate Laura was going, Jamie and Rachel would have plenty of weeding left for them when they returned.

Jamie sat at the kitchen table, reading over her special report assignment. Mrs. Hazelett had circled the last question:

"Imagine that your pencil is alive. What would it do? Where would it go? Write a story about this pencil."

Jamie sighed. Mrs. Hazelett wasn't looking for a short answer.

Rachel came into the kitchen.

"Sara just called me, and I'm going to play at her house tomorrow."

"That sounds fun," Jamie said.

"Yeah, I like going to Sara's," Rachel said. But she didn't look that excited.

"What's wrong?" Jamie asked her.

"I got another letter from Jessica," Rachel said. "And I haven't told her we're not coming back."

Jamie felt her pocket. She hadn't gotten to that in her letter to Sheila either.

"I haven't told Sheila," she said. "I want to know when I'll see her first so I can write that, too."

"Maybe this summer," Rachel said.

"If we take our trip," Jamie said.

"Or maybe Jessica's mom will let her visit Phoenix since we're staying."

Jamie tried to picture Sheila in her new house. They could use the walkie-talkies, and if Celia felt good, they could visit her in her garden.

"Yeah," Jamie said. "I guess we should write them soon so they know."

Rachel slid onto the bench across from Jamie and got her notebook out of her backpack.

Jamie lifted her pencil, thinking about what she wanted to tell Sheila. Then she looked at it. She'd almost forgotten about her story, which she had to read aloud tomorrow morning. She twirled her pencil in her hand, trying to imagine it alive. For one thing, if it could move, it probably wouldn't be sitting in her hand.

"Let's name you Harry," she said to her pencil. She pulled out a sheet of paper and let Harry write the beginning of his adventure.

Jamie's dad came in and glanced over her shoulder.

"Special report, hmmm?" he said. "I thought you were going to start this last week."

"I know," Jamie said. "But don't worry, I know what I'm going to write about." She began writing faster.

Her dad sighed.

"I just hope she's not up all night," he said to Rachel.

Rachel smiled.

"She'll be through way before that," Rachel said. "Right, Jamie?"

Jamie nodded, still writing.

"When she gets through," he whispered to Rachel, "tell her we're going camping this weekend."

Jamie put Harry down.

"Really?" she asked.

"We're thinking of going to an area near Sedona," her dad told her.

Jamie's mom came into the kitchen.

"There's a beautiful river up there," she said. "And the campgrounds will be almost empty this time of year. Everyone else thinks it's too cold."

"Don't they know about snow camping?" Rachel asked.

"Where did you learn about snow camping?" their dad asked her.

"At our old school," she said. "On safety day. We learned about frostbite and this other thing you get where you're so cold you think you're warm."

Their mom laughed.

"I bet safety day is pretty different around here."

Rachel nodded like an expert.

"We had it last week," she said. "They talked about ignoring strangers, and dialing 911 from a pay phone."

Jamie's mom looked at her dad.

"Camping is starting to sound better and better," she said.

Jamie glanced down at her paper. Harry was standing in a beaver pond, waiting.

"Aha," her mom said. "The famous special report. You can read it to us for practice."

"Maybe," Jamie said. No practice would get her ready to read aloud to her class. But ready or not, tomorrow morning she'd be standing alone in the front, telling Harry's adventures.

Chapter Twenty

Jamie sat at her desk, staring at "Harry's Adventures." She sank low in her chair, avoiding Mrs. Hazelett. She tried to make her heart slow down.

"Is that your report?" Elise asked.

Jamie nodded.

"'Harry's Adventures,'" Elise read as she leaned close to Jamie.

"Come on, don't read it," Jamie said.

"The whole class will be hearing it in a minute," Elise said.

Jamie felt her feet get heavier. She wondered how she'd get herself up to the front of the class.

"Don't worry," Elise said. "I bet you write good stories."

"How do you know?" Jamie asked.

Elise shrugged.

"I could tell for sure if you'd just let me read it," she said.

"It's time to share our special reports," Mrs. Hazelett said. "As you know, this quarter you had the option of writing a story to read to the class. Those stories were due today."

Everyone started reaching for their reports.

Paul's hand shot up, as Jamie could have guessed.

"Yes, Paul?" Mrs. Hazelett said.

"Can I go first?" he asked.

"Thank you, but this morning I'm just going to call names," Mrs. Hazelett explained.

Jamie was too far away to read the list, but she didn't need to look to know where her name was.

"Jamie?" Mrs. Hazelett said. "Please bring your report to the front of the room."

Tanya and Stephanie turned around.

"You're reading aloud?" Tanya's eyebrows were raised so high they met her bangs.

Jamie nodded.

"But you never—" Stephanie began.

"Wait till you hear it," Elise said. "It'll be great."

"Don't get too excited," Jamie said, scooting her chair into her desk.

Stephanie turned around. Tanya kept her eyes on Jamie and mouthed "good luck." Jamie smiled. For once she wished she was used to talking as much as Tanya was. She walked to the front of the room.

"You can stand here," Mrs. Hazelett said as she walked to the back of the room. She sat down in a chair, ready to listen with the rest of the class.

Jamie faced the class. She looked out into the rows. Paul was sitting up straight, ready to have something to say after Jamie finished. Scott was slouched next to Paul, probably expecting what he called a "girl story." Melinda was resting her chin in her hands the way she always did when Mrs. Hazelett read out loud. And Elise was nodding, telling her to hurry up.

Jamie glanced at Mrs. Hazelett. She was waiting, her teeth jumping out from behind her lipstick. Jamie remembered the first time she'd seen that lipstick, when Mrs. Hazelett had pounced on her, and she was sure she'd have to tell the whole class about moving from Colorado. This time, from up in front, her face was easier to look at.

"'Harry's Adventures,'" Jamie read.

"Hello, my name is Harry the Pencil. I live in the desk of Melissa Matoria. She is very nice. Her only problem is that she sometimes lends me to her friend Lisa. Lisa is always nervous and bites pencils. All the pencils call being with Lisa 'The Torture Place.'

"It was today that I was lent. I decided to jump out of Lisa's hands and escape out the window with my pal George. Our plan worked. Outside was fun! We climbed up trees. We rolled up and down flagpoles. We visited Toby the Fly. Toby told us to travel on a flying leaf. Our leaf dropped us off in the water of a big lake. We were happy until suddenly beavers started to attack us! We tried to swim but they caught up."

Jamie tried to get herself to slow down. She took a deep breath.

"Come on," Scott said. "What happens to Harry?"

Jamie found her place.

"Then one tried to chew my lead. He spit it out and yelled, 'Hey everybody, don't eat those pencils! They taste awful!' The beavers went away. We were glad.

"Now we missed our home so much that we asked a flying leaf to take us back. We snuck inside the classroom and rolled back to Lisa's desk. She gave us back to Melissa. George and I are going to take another trip after we rest for a while.

"The End."

Jamie put the paper down. She looked out at her class.

"Does anyone have any questions for Jamie?" Mrs. Hazelett asked as she walked to the front of the room.

"How did you think up Harry?" Melinda asked.

Jamie leaned against the board.

"I stared at my own pencil," she said.

"Cool story," Paul said.

"Paul, we're asking for questions," Mrs. Hazelett said. But Jamie thought she saw her smile.

"What happened to the beavers?" Anna asked.

"They're at home in their dam," Jamie said. "But they're planning to find Harry."

"One more question," Mrs. Hazelett said.

Tanya raised her hand.

"Are you going to write a story about that?"

Jamie looked down at her paper.

"Maybe," she said.

"Okay," Mrs. Hazelett said. "Thank you, Jamie. Damon, why don't you come on up."

Jamie walked back to her desk. Her heart was still beating in her throat as she slid into her seat.

"See?" Elise said. "I knew your story would be good."

Jamie glanced down at her story. Before she'd read it, she wasn't sure how it would turn out. But when she'd heard it out loud, she could picture Harry's whole life.

"How did you know?" she asked Elise.

Elise shrugged.

"Some things you just know," she said.

Jamie watched Elise's legs move up and down as she tapped her feet under her desk. She remembered the first time she'd caught a glimpse of those red shorts, under Elise's pencil, then hidden in the tree.

"Some things are like that," Jamie said.

They sat back in their chairs, together in silence, waiting for Damon to begin.

Chapter Twenty-One

Jamie lay in bed, watching the wires above her shift back and forth. She tried to rock herself to sleep the way Rachel was, but it didn't work. She turned over and hugged her pillow. She lay perfectly still, hoping for a dream to take over. But her pillow felt too warm against her head. Finally she sat up.

Jamie stared out her window from her bed. The moon lit up the back wall of their yard, making it glow between the darkness of the sky and the grass below. The wall seemed bare and quiet, but wide awake. The mountains used to look that way, after the snow fell, light blue and glowing against the night sky. But there was no chance for snow here.

Jamie stood up silently and walked to the window. She

leaned against it, staring at the wall. Then she noticed the bottom of the wall. It looked like it was moving up and down, floating in the grass. Jamie squinted. Actually, it looked more like the grass was an ocean lapping against the wall.

"Rachel!" Jamie whispered. "Wake up!"

"I was almost asleep," Rachel groaned.

"You've been sleeping for hours," Jamie said, still staring out the window.

Rachel rolled off her bed and fell to the floor.

"What is it?" she asked.

"Irrigation!" Jamie said. "We've missed it every time, and now it's here."

She ran from the window to their door and led Rachel down the hallway, through the kitchen. Carefully, she unhitched the back door.

"Come on," she whispered.

She pushed up the sleeves of her nightshirt and stepped into the dark water. It surrounded the bottom of her legs. She bent down and ran her fingers through it. It felt warm, and the grass was softer than usual underneath it.

Rachel ran past her and did a cartwheel through the water. Jamie followed, showering Rachel as she went.

"It's a storm!" Rachel said, lifting waves of water up to spray Jamie.

Jamie spun in circles, making the water fly.

"There are frogs and crawdads in here," she told Rachel. "We just can't see them."

"Maybe we could if we sat up on the wall," Rachel said.

They wiped their feet on the wall's edge. Jamie went first, putting her fingers in cracks and pulling herself up to stand on small ledges. The wall was old enough to offer lots of places to grab. Jamie scrambled up on the top and watched Rachel, guiding her to the easier cracks. Soon Rachel sat beside her.

"Look," Rachel said, peering down at the bottom of the wall. "Three baby frogs."

Jamie stared closely. She saw two of them dart, jumping in and out of the water.

"They're so small," Rachel said.

"Yeah," Jamie said, "especially from here."

They leaned back, listening to the quiet. A single croak drifted through it, and soon the air was alive with answers, croaks of all kinds sounding in the dark.

Jamie looked up. The moon was far above them now, outshining all the houses, hiding the stars, the desert,

South Mountain, and even the busy streets under its light.

Rachel lay on top of the wall.

"It's a moon bath," she said.

Jamie lay with her head near Rachel's, feeling the moon-light drift toward them, making them glow in the warm Phoenix air.